OTHER SIDE OF LOVE

A DIFFERENT KIND OF LOVE ROMANCE: SARAH AND BENNY

LIZ DURANO

to my Lucas

You are one amazing and beautiful boy. I am so grateful to
be your mother.

FOREWORD

Sarah and Benny first appeared during the family dinner scene in *Everything She Ever Wanted* with their son Dyami. From the first moment they appeared on the page, I always knew there was more to their story, one that would span over a decade. It would make the decision to write their story difficult because I've always seen authors write in a linear fashion, moving forward instead of going back. That's how *Every Breath*, their Valentine's Day slice-of-life novella came to be.

But it wasn't enough.

For what made Sarah and Benny special was their past, and after struggling to move forward with more stories in the series, I knew the reason I couldn't was because I had to go back in time and tell theirs first.

As it was, I couldn't write anything else anyway and I'm glad I finally decided to let the characters do the talking. For the moment I started writing their story, nothing has ever felt so right and I hope you'll feel the same way.

I hope you enjoy *Other Side of Love*. This is Sarah and Benny's story...

In beauty I walk
With beauty before me I walk
With beauty behind me I walk
With beauty above me I walk
With beauty around me I walk
It has become beauty again
It has become beauty again
It has become beauty again
It has become beauty again

~"The Beauty Way"
Navajo/Diné traditional prayer

CHAPTER ONE

Sarah

"VISITING YOUR FAMILY AFTER THIS?"

I turn to see Melina, the nurse supervisor writing down notes on the whiteboard behind the nurses' station. With my shift ending in five minutes, she's setting up the room assignment chart for the next shift.

"Yup, after my run and a quick nap." I stifle a yawn as I get up from the counter, the last twelve hours finally getting to me but not until after my run. Gotta get the miles in and then I can fall asleep.

"Damn, girl. I don't know how you can still run after the night I heard you guys had," she says, shaking her head. "Or any night shift for that matter."

I chuckle, rolling my eyes as the other staff members chime in to express their amazement. After all, twelve-hour shifts are no joke but with the joggers I see along the irrigation canal behind the medical center, it's not like I'm alone enjoying the outdoors. And with the last few hours being the way they were, I need the distraction—a gunshot wound, a barroom brawl resulting in stitches, two drunk driver-related car accidents resulting in broken bones and one fatality. I try not to think of that last one. Some nights, nothing much happens at all in the Emergency Room.

Still, it's just another day as a travel nurse in Shiprock, New Mexico. If I thought this job was going to be a piece of cake, I was fooling myself. But I already knew it wouldn't be easy and that's why I took it. As long as it was far enough away from civilization and close enough to Taos that I could drive there during my days off, it was good enough for me. Better than being all alone in the middle of nowhere without family close by. Been there, done that and I'm not doing that again.

"Did you call Enrico back yet?" Melina asks as she settles behind the front desk. She's only been trying to get me to go out with her son ever since he met me while dropping something off for his mother two weeks ago. Why did I even agree to have Melina give him my phone number when I have no plans on dating anyone at the moment. It hasn't been on the agenda for the past year, and at the rate my love life has been going, not anytime soon. I'm so done with men that I'm ready to live the rest of my life alone.

"I haven't had time, Mel," I say, slipping on my cardigan. "Between work and driving to Taos each weekend, I've been busy. Anyway, I'm going to clock–"

The front doors slide open and two men stride in,

one cradling a bloody arm and the other looking at his companion nervously, one of the lenses of his wire-rimmed glasses cracked.

"Linda's not here yet," Melina says, turning to look at the new arrivals. "Can you stay five more minutes?"

I barely hear Melina, not when my attention is riveted to the tall man with intense brown eyes and a trimmed beard. As he storms into the clinic, his button-down shirt barely hides the outline of his muscled chest and a flat stomach. A hint of a tattoo peeks from under the collar of his shirt and around his neck, a silver ring hangs from a silver chain. He's wearing two other chains although one looks like male beads. And then there are his rings. He's wearing at least three but as my gaze drifts to his hands, I know for sure that his index fingers will be bare.

Only when a Navajo is dead, he'd told me almost three years ago.

Sure enough, as I glance at his hands, his pointer fingers are free of rings.

Suddenly the tall man stops in his tracks, his eyes narrowing at the sight of me as his companion approaches the counter.

"Colton Johnson, Ma'am, and this here's Doctor Benny Turner," Benny's tall blond-haired companion says. "We were out surveying and the truck rolled. The doc here got a gash to his–"

"The truck didn't roll," Benny grumbles as he looks

away from me and approaches the counter. "You went off the damn embankment and nearly killed us both."

"Sarah, hang on a sec," Melina says as she retrieves a clipboard from the wall slot with the intake forms for new patients to fill out.

"I thought it was just a little dip on the road," says Colton as Benny scoffs.

"Dip on the road, my ass. You need a better prescription for your–"

"Alright, gentlemen, no arguing in my lobby," Melina says sternly. "Why don't we get you two in the room and have that arm looked at?" She turns to Benny. "That's a nasty bump on that forehead. Did you hit your head?"

Benny scowls as he rubs his head with his uninjured hand. "No."

"Yeah, he hit the dashboard," the other man says as Benny glowers at him even more, the red spot on his forehead turning even redder. "You weren't wearing your seatbelt, man. You were checking your phone."

"True, but I was also in the process of putting it on when you stepped on the gas."

"I thought I'd–"

"Alright, that's it," Melina says sternly. "Room five is available. You guys are lucky we're not too busy right–"

Melina doesn't finish what she says for a woman with a screaming baby rushes through the double doors followed by a woman pushing an older man in a wheelchair.

"I got this. Sir?" I ask politely as I take the patient

folder from Melina. With Colton not needing any medical attention, that leaves only Benny and unless I want him to bleed all over the lobby, I need to get him into an examination room.

Across the counter, Colton points to an empty chair in the lobby. "I'll wait for you out here, man."

"Whatever," Benny mutters as I press the button to unlock the door separating the lobby from the rest of the clinic.

"Follow me." As I make my way down the hallway to the examination room, I see the clock turn 7:00 AM. Oh well, there go my plans for a quick run followed by a stop at the local restaurant for a breakfast burrito, a nap and then the three-hour drive to Taos. What's a few more minutes until Linda gets here to start her shift?

"How long have you been working here?" Benny asks under his breath as he follows me to Room Five.

"Since nine last night."

He glares at me and I sigh, pointing to the examination table. "Two months. Anyway, why don't you sit down and we'll get your paperwork started before the nurse gets here."

"But I thought you were my nurse."

"Lucky you, I was just finishing my shift," I reply coolly, avoiding his gaze. "So I'm just filling in until Nurse Linda gets here."

Benny doesn't answer. He studies me, an amused expression on his face. "Two months... man, I should have gotten banged up sooner if I'd known you were here. But then, I've been out of town."

"Sit down, Mr. Turner," I say, motioning toward the chair next to the examination table. "I'll need to take down your information before the doctor gets here."

It takes me five minutes to get all Benny's information down even if I know half of it already. Too bad the half that I know about him has no place in a medical chart like the fact that he earned his Master's in Environmental Sciences from the University of New Mexico in Albuquerque while I was completing my Bachelors in Nursing or that he loves anything homemade, like hominy stew and carne adovado.

"You still running?" Benny asks, studying my face. "You got color on you like you have."

"Then I probably have been running," I say dryly. He'd know. He was the one who introduced me to running outdoors back during our time at UNM, getting me hooked to the feel of the sun and the wind on my face, the earth at my feet, and the sight of cacti, sagebrush, and the occasional petroglyph in the distance.

He doesn't speak for a few moments, his eyes narrowing as he studies my face, a faint grin on his lips. "You must be the new nurse they were talking about. One of my other guys had to be brought in a few weeks ago. Got a nasty gash on his leg while surveying."

I take the stethoscope from around my neck and place the ear tips in my ears. "Do you always scope out every one of the nurses around here?"

"Only the ones I already know," Benny says as I twist the ear tips slightly to make a good seal, his voice becoming muffled as he continues. "Anyway, they have a pretty high turnover rate at this place since it's on the rez and so I'm grateful for every person who does show up. The locals around here need people like you."

"Take a deep breath."

Benny does as he's told and then exhales. As I rest the diaphragm on another spot on his chest, I can't help but notice how defined his pectoral muscles are. And then there's the hint of a six-pack underneath his white shirt. He definitely still works out.

"Come to think of it, I don't know why you're doing that when it's just my arm that's injured," he says as if noticing my gaze and I clear my throat.

"Your friend said you hit your head."

"True, but my head's up here," he says, pointing to his temple, "not where your stethoscope thing is at."

"Don't worry. I'll get there soon enough and find out if there's anything between your ears."

"Ouch," he says, still grinning as I roll my eyes and decide he's healthy as an ox and lift the diaphragm away from his chest.

"You haven't changed, you know that? You're still incorrigible."

"Now that's pretty harsh, isn't it? We haven't seen each other in, what? Two years?" Benny says. "Too long, if you ask me."

"Not long enough, actually." I loop the stethoscope

over my neck. "I should have checked to see if you worked here before I took the job."

This time, he doesn't answer right away, his eyes narrowing as he studies me. For a moment, I wonder if I've gone too far. But before I can apologize, Benny cracks a smile. "Glad to see you're still feisty as ever, Sarah Drexel. I like that."

The sound of my name escaping his lips makes my heart quicken and I get up abruptly, the chair rolling away and hitting the wall. Wouldn't you know it? Obviously, two years isn't long enough to get rid of my body's reaction to Benny Turner saying my name, certainly not after that night I told him my secrets. I'd almost forgotten how it sounded coming from him with his baritone voice. But I can't allow myself to be distracted right now, not when I've got a job to do.

"Why don't we fix that nasty boo-boo and get you on your way, Mr. Turner?" I say as sweetly as I can just as the door opens and the doctor steps inside the room.

"Ah, Nurse Sarah, could you stay and help me with Mr. Turner here?" the doctor asks. "Linda is doing intake on the new patient and she should be here shortly."

As I nod and tell the doctor it's okay, I don't miss seeing Benny's grin widen, as if happy that I'm stuck with him. He really shouldn't be smiling, not when we didn't exactly end up on good terms two years ago. If I could wipe Benny's grin off his face I would, but that would probably only make my problems worse.

After all, he's not the one who said the things she

shouldn't have said the last time we were together two years ago. That was the night I was so drunk out of my head I asked Benny to do things I'd never asked any man to do before.

But that night, I learned firsthand that everyone had their limits and to my shame, Benny drew the line he'd never cross...not even with me.

———

AN HOUR LATER, my run along the irrigation ditch behind the medical center done, my phone rings as I get behind the wheel of my SUV. I don't need to see who's calling. Even though I'm three hours away from Taos, nothing makes my mother happier than knowing I'm back in the same state where I grew up.

"You finished with work, mija?"

"Just got done with my run and now heading home for a nap." It's really a four-hour nap, if anything, but I doubt I'll be able to do that now that I can't get Benny out of my mind. Haven't thought of anything else throughout my run either. How could he act like that last night we spent together never happened?

"I can't wait to see you today," Mom says, her words breaking through my thoughts. "Make sure you're well-rested before you leave the house, okay? The highway can be crazy."

I turn the key in the ignition, allowing the car to warm up. "I will."

There's a pause and I have a feeling she's got something else to say but she's holding back. "Your dad is flying in tonight. Thought you should know considering the last time you both talked, you ended up leaving earlier than you'd planned."

I take a deep breath. The last time Dad and I saw each other we had an argument and I walked out of the house. I couldn't handle the things he said about my last relationship and he couldn't stop himself from being too direct, wanting only to fix the problem, as he saw it.

For Mom's birthday two months ago, I told her I was working the moment I knew Dad was flying in and that I couldn't visit until I was on my day off which happened to be the day Dad had to return to New York. It wasn't true, of course, but I wasn't ready to face him just as I'm not ready to face him tonight either. I hate letting him down and for being a major fuck-up twice in a row.

And always with a man.

"Why don't I call you later, Mom, after I take my nap?" I say, not wanting to think about Dad anymore. "We had a crazy shift last night and I just want to crawl into bed."

"Alright, mija. Te amo."

"Te amo, Mom. I'll see you in a few hours, okay?" But even as I hang up, I know I won't. I'll call her later and tell her that one of the nurses is out sick and that the clinic needs me to come in tonight.

She'll understand why.

CHAPTER TWO

Benny

SMALL WORLD. WHO'D HAVE THOUGHT SARAH Drexel would be working right here in Shiprock? Hell, I didn't, not in a million years, not after she pretended I didn't exist after two years of friendship. Not that I intended to mention that little detail with the doctor present and Sarah clearly focusing on the job at hand, refusing to meet my eyes the whole time.

I first met her at a coffee shop in Albuquerque four years ago when she was studying Nursing and I was working toward my Masters in Environmental Sciences. The place was packed and she and another friend asked if they could sit at my table since I was hogging one all to myself. I almost said no but figured, what the heck, I was going to leave in five minutes anyway and head to the university library where it would be quieter. I also needed to use the printer.

Before I knew it, five minutes turned to ten and then

ten turned into two hours. Sarah's dark blue eyes and fiery passion intrigued me as she advocated for the imaginary patient she and her friend were assigned to treat for a case study who happened to be Navajo. While her friend was all for drugs, Sarah wanted to know the why's of the patient's illness. Family history, current diet, and nutrition. She even included their culture even if the things she said were probably lifted off some history book she just read.

"Let's say they're hooked on those fry breads that we all know about, the ones that we drizzle with honey and sugar—"

"Navajo tacos!" Her friend exclaimed as Sarah nodded.

"Did you know that flour, sugar, and lard were never a normal part of the Native American's diet?" Sarah continued. "It was given to them by the government when they were forced into the reservation. What the heck can you make with all that flour, lard, and sugar and nothing else? The stuff was also rotten and old. So they got creative, and that's how fry bread came to be."

"You make it sound like they had a choice," I'd said and they both looked in my direction as if just realizing I'd never left. "I wouldn't say that they're 'hooked' on fry bread, certainly not back then. It was either that or starvation and as it were, thousands had already died along the way. Before they were forced from their lands to go on the Long Walk to Hwéeldi, the Place of Suffering, my people grew their own vegetables and beans and basically had a very healthy diet. Thanks to all that flour, lard, and sugar they gave us, and the fact that we're given land that's not exactly sustainable except for uranium or coal, diabetes, hypertension, and obesity have been on the rise among my people for as long as fry bread came to be."

I can't forget the look I got from her as she lifted her chin and said, "Excuse me, but who the hell are you?"

"Benjamin Turner, Ma'am," I replied. "Navajo, or as we call ourselves, Diné."

"But you're not really full Navajo, are you?" she asked, her brow furrowing as she brought her hand to her jaw. "You don't look..."

"My mother is full Navajo or Diné and my father's Caucasian... with a bit of Spanish mixed in there as well," I replied, pointing to my beard. "What about you?"

There was that chin tilt again. "New Mexican. Proud and true."

Her friend looked at her, frowning. "But your dad's a New Yorker. You're only half."

"I grew up here, so that makes me New Mexican," Sarah said defiantly as her friend shrugged.

I don't even remember her friend's name—Amy or Alannah or Allison—for all I saw was Sarah. It felt like I'd been hit by a bolt of lightning whenever she looked at me, meeting my gaze boldly. Not a lot of women on campus did that and I liked that about her. Smart, feisty, proud.

But there was something different with the Sarah I

saw at the clinic. There was still that feisty part of her, true, but there was also something else that I can't place, an undercurrent I saw only once before, the last night she and I were together.

Regret? Shame?

Whatever it was, I'd never know for the entire time Sarah cleaned up my wound, she never looked me in the eye. The doctor was also busy talking about side-effects although I barely heard what he was saying. I just wanted Sarah to lift her gaze and look at me, really look at me. But she never did. As far as everyone at the clinic was concerned, we'd never met before today.

The moment the other nurse entered the room, Sarah got up and left and my sour mood returned immediately. It worsened when I emerged from the back office, my arm stitched and wrapped in a bandage, and I spotted Colton in the waiting room typing away on his laptop.

Whose idea was it for me to mentor this kid again, and so soon after I got back from being out on the field for the last three weeks? I needed a break, for crying out loud, not some city kid to babysit around the reservation.

And what was the deal with me letting him get behind the wheel when the kid easily panicked at the sight of a coyote? And panic he did, drove us right over the damn embankment and we're lucky all we got was a gash in my arm and a bump on my head.

But as Colton and I step outside and head back to the work truck, its bumper sitting in the flatbed, I really can't complain. It got us into the clinic where I ran into Sarah

Drexel two years after she decided we couldn't be friends anymore.

AT THE OFFICE, I change my shirt and get to work. I really don't have much to do, just a bunch of reports to review for tomorrow's meeting and phone calls to make. There's also a call I need to return from my mother who left a message ten minutes ago. She and my stepfather live in the Navajo Nation with my half-twin brothers Tahoma and Tsela. Up until two months ago, my half-sister Marjorie lived there, too, but she's since moved into her own apartment near the Diné College where she's working on a degree in Elementary Education with a major in Diné Studies. Like Noelle Descheney, Marjorie wants to stay in the Navajo Nation.

At the thought of my ex-girlfriend, I glance at my phone, my thumb hovering over my mother's cell phone number. There's actually no reception at home but whenever she drives into town, she finds the best spot to make her calls. Right about now, she should be at the store waiting for me to call her back in case I'm available. I know she wishes I lived back on the homestead with her but with all the work and traveling I do, often on short notice, living in the city is a more ideal arrangement for me.

But as I stare at her phone number on the display, I know I'm delaying the inevitable. I already know what she's going to say if I call her back right now and if I don't, when I come home.

Have you called Noelle yet? It's been four weeks since you told me you were going to get back together and finally ask her to marry you. It's been six years, Benny. The poor girl can't wait forever.

I exhale. Of course, Mother's got a point. And it's not just Noelle who's been waiting for me to make up my mind. It's both our families who have known each other for generations. We basically grew up together. She even taught me how to dance and sure enough, I ended up dancing in one of the Navajo Nation fairs with her. I was only ten then and she was nine, but no one will let us live that one down. We've been matched ever since.

But just because everyone else thought we were a perfect match didn't mean Noelle and I felt the same way—or that's what I've told myself every time I've suggested we cool off. Back then, she knew my desire to go to college and be just like my late dad who was an engineer for a company in Roswell. And it wasn't just me. Noelle wanted to go to college, too, earn her degree in Diné studies and return to the reservation to teach the native kids. And so right after high school, we agreed to put education first. We weren't seriously dating then but we were exclusive enough. But we also knew that we could be the first ones from our families to finish college and that's exactly what happened.

That's when we became exclusive—in a way—but also on and off since I attended college in Florida and it wasn't really easy to be completely "on." After college, I went straight to grad school and she did, too.

Only this time, I can't blame the delay on education. I've taken every damn thing I could take. I've got a Doctorate now and it's time to go to work. It's also time to get married and have kids. I'm twenty-nine and Noelle is a year younger than me. High time to get married, as Mother would say every time I came home to help around the homestead. When Noelle gave me the ultimatum two months ago—propose or break up—I chose the latter. I wasn't ready then and I'm still not ready.

So why the hell did I tell my entire family that I'd get back with Noelle and finally ask her to marry me four weeks ago? Sure, I got tired of them asking the same question every time I went home but that didn't mean I had to say something I didn't mean. Or maybe I did then, my desire to be the good son and Navajo overtaking every rational thought. Too bad rational thought is hard to come by right now, too, not when all I can think about is Sarah and what she's doing on the reservation, of all places. Exhaling, I put my phone back inside my desk drawer. I'll call Mother later.

By noon, the arm that got the tetanus vaccine starts to throb and I'm suddenly not feeling too great. I've got a headache and my body is hurting all over. I retrieve the paper bag the nurse gave me before I left the clinic, remembering she'd put a piece of paper that listed all the side-effects on top of the prescription strength painkillers I'm supposed to take. I never bothered to read about the side-effects but now I need to make sure it's not my imagination.

Most common side effects include redness and swelling around the injection site. Body aches. Fever. Headache.

Great. Looks like I've got all the side-effects down pat. I rub my temples, wishing the dull throbbing would ease off. I look up to see Colton typing reports and turn off my laptop. Hell, let the kid continue working until five. I'm done.

"You heading out early, Benny?" Tony asks as I slip my laptop into my backpack. He's one of the specialists who works with me, a fellow Diné.

"Yup. Gonna go home and rest. I need to be up early tomorrow for that meeting at the main office."

"Got someone to keep an eye on you? That's a nasty bruise you've got on your forehead."

I scoff. "You volunteering?"

"Heck no, man," he says, laughing. "Get someone else. I'm taken."

Normally, I'd have a good comeback for Tony but not right now. I've got a throbbing headache. "Alright, I'm out. See you guys next week."

I grab my backpack and sling it over my shoulder. I need to head to the supermarket first before going home. With a fridge that probably only has a six-pack of beer and leftovers from last night's dinner with the guys from work, I'm going to need to do some shopping. Either I have to figure out how to get food delivered to my apartment regularly or I need to learn how to cook.

I curse under my breath when my arm starts to throb again during the drive to City Market on Highway 64. It'd probably be a good idea to add a painkiller or two to the list of things I need to buy. I don't like them and hardly use them, but at this point, it doesn't hurt to have some on hand. I'm also wishing I had someone with me just in case the doctor's right about me having some kind of a concussion from when my head hit the dashboard. I'd refused additional tests, not when it meant having to drive to another part of the medical center to get them. Besides, with Sarah gone, the thrill was pretty much gone, too. I just wanted to get out of there.

By the time I turn into the parking lot, my mental list of things to pick up has grown even longer. Laundry soap, dryer sheets, soup mix. Hatch green chili sauce— and the best kind at that, if they have it in case I start acting crazy and actually want to make something from scratch. But with me feeling like crap, I'll probably just pick up a few microwave-ready meals instead.

That's when I see her and my heart rate speeds up. How the hell did I miss bumping into her the last two months? But that's what happens when the last time I've gone shopping was over two months ago and the last three weeks I've been out of town.

No longer wearing scrubs, Sarah looks great in a dark blue sleeveless top over faded jeans, her long hair falling over her shoulders as she loads her groceries in the trunk of her SUV. Her curves are to die for and our eyes meet when I park my truck in the only available spot right next to her SUV. As she scowls, I can't stop grinning. It's as if my facial muscles have a will of their own, matching the butterflies that suddenly come to life in my belly. Two years after she left without saying goodbye, turns out I still have a secret crush on Sarah Drexel.

I also don't remember a single thing I'm supposed to get inside the store. Not a damn thing.

CHAPTER THREE

Sarah

FOR SOMEONE I HAVEN'T SEEN SINCE I MOVED HERE two months ago, I suddenly can't turn around without bumping into Benny Turner. In this case, twice on the same day. Is that why my heart is beating as if I've just completed a sprint?

"Hey," I say as he gets out of his truck. His left arm is bandaged just above the elbow, the wrap peeking from under the folded sleeve of his button-down shirt which also reveals his muscled forearm, tribal tattoos gracing his skin. As I force myself to look up, his expression looks pinched like he's hurting. "Tetanus shot bothering you?"

"How'd you know?"

"Standard operating procedure. It's the big guys who usually feel the aches and pains the most." I place the last of my purchases into the trunk of my SUV and close the door. Since I canceled my plans to drive down to Taos, it meant a trip to the supermarket as soon as I woke up from my nap to stock up on junk food and rent a DVD. Maybe some action flick or comedy, anything that will take my mind off Benny and his six-pack abs. Only that's not exactly working because he's right in front of me and just to be sure, I might need to go back inside and get new batteries.

"Did you just come from the office?" I ask as Benny rubs his bandaged arm absently. "I would have thought you took the rest of the day off. That cut was nasty, and that bump on your noggin was, too."

"It's nothing," he grunts and I can't help but chuckle. Benny hasn't changed much even if he's looking a bit pale. Side-effects must be hitting him hard.

"It's normal for patients to feel pain and even get a fever, muscle aches, nausea. Even lightheadedness," I say. "In fact, you probably shouldn't be driving."

"Nobody told me that at the clinic," he says, frowning.

"I'm sure they did. You just didn't hear them."

Benny's eyes narrow as he studies me, as if figuring out if I'm serious. Then he shrugs. "Maybe they did, maybe they didn't. I'm a big boy."

"That you are. But acetaminophen should ease the pain. Not that I'm officially diagnosing or prescribing you anything," I say.

"Don't worry. I won't tell anyone."

"What about a bit of TLC from your girlfriend?" I continue, almost saying Noelle's name but knowing I'd be pushing it if I did. At the very least, he's not wearing a ring. "I'm sure she could—"

"I don't have a girlfriend."

I look at Benny incredulously. *Benny Turner? Single? Did hell just freeze over? What about Noelle?*

But before I can say anything else, I stop myself. It's really none of my business if he has a girlfriend or not. I also need to stop worrying about Benny. Before we know it, I'll be offering to make him dinner and tucking him into bed. I walk past him and pull open the driver side door of my SUV.

"I should get going. It was nice seeing you again, Benny." I do my best to act nonchalant even as my heart thunders inside my chest. How can two years go by and yet feel like it was yesterday when I last saw him?

"Likewise, Sarah," he says as I get behind the wheel.

He closes the driver side door for me and as I slip the key in the ignition, I lower the window. "Go home and get some rest, Benny. A fever reducer and painkiller along with chicken noodle soup should do you some good, too."

He rests his hands on the door. "Green chili maybe?"

I nod, gazing at his empty ring finger before forcing myself to look at his face. "Yeah, green chili stew although I'd opt for something clearer. And rest. Lots of rest."

For a moment Benny doesn't speak though a faint smile lingers on his lips. Then he takes a deep breath, taps my door two times, and steps away. "Thanks for all your help, Sarah. Guess I'll see you around," he says, turning away from me and grabbing the basket I'd parked by the side of my SUV.

As I turn the ignition, I know Benny's too tough to admit he needs help. At the same time, I've got no excuse treating him the way I just did especially when we used to be good friends in college. I'm a nurse, for crying out loud. I'm supposed to be compassionate.

I chuckle to myself as I start the engine. Yeah, right. Compassionate, my ass. But as I rest my hand on the gear shift, there's no denying the feelings that I used to feel for Benny are now rushing back like water breaking through a dam.

I shift the gear in reverse, reminding myself that the last thing I need is another complication in my life. The sooner I nip the idea of reconnecting with Benny in the bud, the better it is for both of us.

SO MUCH FOR WALKING AWAY.

Five minutes later, I find Benny in the medicine aisle, standing between the ibuprofen and acetaminophen products and holding one in each hand. Tall and broad-shouldered, Benny has always been a sight to behold. It's in the way he carries himself, raw confidence evident in every step and a roughness underneath the surface.

Right now, though, it's a different story. Benny looks

tired and a bit confused as he tries to decide which bottle of pills to buy. But I can't blame him. Benny's not the type to rely on medication. He's the type of man to power through broken bones and barroom brawls, two things I've witnessed when we were both students at UNM. But body aches and fever from a tetanus shot? Apparently not so much.

"Alright, any more of this looking like a lost puppy and I'll be taking you home. Why don't we get you all sorted out?" I take the box of ibuprofen from his hand and return it to the shelf. When he doesn't say anything, I continue, "Do you live far from here?"

"No, but I thought you were going home."

"I changed my mind."

He shrugs. "I'm not a charity case, Sarah. I'm fine."

"Of course, I know that. But if you want, I can help you with whatever you need to buy and follow you to your apartment. We'll get you settled and I'll make you something to eat."

He looks unconvinced. "You don't have to do that."

"Alright then," I say, turning away. "Just say the word then and I'll be on my way."

Benny opens his mouth to say something but stops. Then he nods. "Alright, nurse Sarah, I'll take you up on your offer, but you better not be doing this out of pity."

"Not out of pity, no," I reply, pushing his basket down the aisle. "As a friend... a former friend or whatever the hell we ended up as after I... well, whatever." I take a deep breath. "Anyway, I'd rather you not go home alone, not when you look the way you do and it'd be nice to have some company tonight. Maybe we can catch up on what we've both been up to."

He arches an eyebrow. "That's all?"

"I was going to visit my family in Taos but since my Dad's in town, I figured I'd give Mom space to be with him."

Benny looks at me, his eyes narrowing. "There are twenty-four hours in a day, Sarah. Surely she'll have time to spend with you while you're there."

"Dad comes in every two weeks to visit her," I say, my excuse sounding thin. "I figured I'd give them time to be alone."

"He still live in New York while your mom and brother live in Taos?"

I nod. "Yup.

"And they're not separated or anything? Divorced?"

I shake my head as he stops in front of the meat aisle. "Hell no. They just have this weird arrangement where he works there but flies back to Taos twice a month, spends time with Mom, Nana, and Dax and then flies back again. It's crazy."

"Why does he do that?"

"Because he handles other people's money and he loves what he does. Mom would like him to work from Taos but big money's back east, you know?" I pause, choosing two packets each of precut pork shoulder and pork belly and putting them in the basket. I don't know why I'm telling him my life story all of a sudden. But then, there was a time when we used to have the same exact conversations. "Anyway, I don't know if you remember, but my dad owns an investment firm that handles rich people's money."

Benny nods. "I remember. I met him the night you graduated. He didn't like me too much."

"He doesn't like any guy being within ten feet of me," I say, chuckling dryly. "Anyway, his business has gotten pretty successful that it allows him to charter a plane on weekends if he has to." As I speak, I notice the furrow on Benny's brow as he studies the stuff I've put inside his basket.

"You're making hominy stew?" he asks and I can spy the hint of a smile on his face.

"Why not? It's your favorite, isn't it? You'll just have to settle for frozen hominy as the base. I don't intend on soaking dried hominy overnight."

"You're welcome to," he says as I glare at him. "Alright, frozen is fine. It's better than canned."

"I don't know if you've got spices in your kitchen–"

"Salt and pepper count?"

"–so I'm going to get everything just to be sure." I stop in front of the spices aisle and take a jar of cumin seeds, Mexican oregano, and bay leaf from the shelf and toss them into the basket. "That okay with you?"

He grins, nodding. "You're the boss."

"And I'm just going to make this for you, make sure you're not running a high fever or anything, and then leave, okay?" As the words leave my mouth, it almost seems like I'm trying to convince myself that's all I want to do. After all, this is me being the compassionate person I really am underneath all the armor I need to wear around Benny, even as the broad grin on his face makes my belly do flip flops.

"Alright," Benny says, grimacing as he rubs his bicep before stifling a yawn. "Deal it is."

I follow him to his apartment and help him with the groceries. He tells me it's a fully furnished long-term rental, one he uses when he's in town since he's mostly assigned in the Taos office. But with his last assignment sending him to Colorado on a weekly basis, it was better to simply stay in Shiprock.

After taking a painkiller, Benny sits on the couch to watch me prepare dinner, yawning until he falls asleep while I'm chopping the onions and garlic, his boots still on his feet. I wake him up just long enough to help him get them off and cover him with a blanket I retrieve from his bed.

"I really should help you," he says, yawning.

"Nope. Your job is to rest right now." I lay the blanket over him. "In case you've forgotten, you hit your head and you cut your arm this morning. The adrenaline has pretty much worn off after your grand adventure and that's one of the reasons you're tired. So rest."

He smiles. "Is that an order, Nurse Sarah?"

"Yes, it is." I wish I could stop myself from grinning as I make my way back to the kitchen and wash my hands but it's useless. Having Benny in the same room with me is making me feel giddy. "Now sleep and don't worry about me. The stew will take some time to cook anyway."

Benny rubs his eyes. "Will you stay and have dinner with me? It would suck to eat it all alone. I'll take care of the clean-up."

Suddenly I feel silly thinking I'd leave as soon as dinner was ready. Who am I fooling. "Alright, but only if you go to sleep, Benny. I'll be right here."

This time he doesn't reply and it doesn't take long for him to fall asleep the moment he closes his eyes, his uninjured arm draped over his eyes. The poor guy is exhausted. The tetanus shot got him good and it didn't help that he went straight to work after the whole incident with the truck. He should have gone home.

But if he did, then I wouldn't have run into him at the store and I certainly wouldn't be in his kitchen right now. And for the first time since I started working in Shiprock, I'm actually happy, almost content as I get everything ready for the hominy stew—jalapeños, chiles, tomato and pork join the onions and garlic in the pot along with the hominy I'd defrosted in the microwave. It'll take awhile for the meat to soften but I figure Benny will be out for about two hours or so, just enough time for the stew to almost be ready.

Hopefully, it'll be enough time for the butterflies in my belly to settle down, too.

CHAPTER FOUR

Benny

I DON'T MEAN TO FALL ASLEEP AS SOON AS WE ARRIVE at my apartment but that's exactly what happens the moment I sit down on my couch after downing the two pills Sarah hands me. Whatever stuff they put in those tetanus vaccines, it's strong enough to make me feel like shit but thank God there's stuff to counter that. Sarah also tells me that it's more likely all that adrenaline from this morning's incident finally wore off and my body just needs to rest. If she meant the excitement of seeing her again, she's probably right.

"What time is it?" I ask when I wake up.

"About seven. You were out like a light after you took the Tylenol. But you should feel even better when you get something in you," she says as I get up from the couch. "You look better than you did earlier, that's for sure. You've got some color back."

"That bad, eh?"

She chuckles. "Not really. You were looking just a little pale, something I'm not used to seeing."

"In that case, I better pretty myself up for dinner." I head to the bathroom to wash my face, brushing my teeth for good measure. Then I take a good look at my reflection in the mirror. Sarah's right about one thing. I do have some color back and I feel better. The headache's gone, too. Now I just need to get homemade food inside me.

The aroma of hominy stew fills my apartment and makes my stomach growl the moment I emerge from the bathroom. Sarah is kneading dough in a bowl when I join her in the kitchen.

"You didn't have to make fry bread," I say, grabbing a kitchen towel from the cupboard and setting it on the counter. She'll need it to cover the bowl for the dough to rest before frying.

"You on a diet?"

I chuckle, shaking my head. "Do I need to be on one?"

Sarah eyes me, her gaze traveling down my torso before moving back up to my face. "No, and it's not like you didn't already know that. You work out."

"Looks like you do, too," I say as she sets the ball of dough in the glass bowl and lays the towel over it. She lifts the lid of the pot and my stomach growls again as steam escapes.

"I really appreciate you keeping me company."

"You don't talk much so that's a plus. Here, taste it and let me know what you think," she says as I take a spoon and dip it into the pot. I taste it, closing my eyes as the flavors explode in my mouth.

"Wow." I hand the spoon to her and she gently tastes the remaining half. She thinks for a moment and nods.

"You're right. It tastes good although it probably needs another hour for the meat to be really tender. But for now, it will do in a pinch."

"I don't think I can wait another hour," I say, patting my stomach. "I haven't had anything since this morning."

"Half an hour then," she says, laughing. "I still have to prepare the fry bread."

"Need help?"

"You can set the table," she says as she sets the lid back on the pot. "The posole should be done by the time I cook the fry bread."

I open the windows to let the apartment air circulate, the stars already lighting up the sky. In the distance, lightning flashes followed by thunder. Just another light show in New Mexico, something Sarah and I used to enjoy watching back when we lived in Albuquerque. We used to pull the couch in front of the window, prop our feet up on the ledge and talk about anything and everything... except anything related to dating.

And here we are again. Friends but not exactly friends, both of us almost cautious as we navigate around each other in the kitchen, trying not to touch, doing our best not to look.

"Dinner's ready," Sarah announces and I pull a chair for her and wait for her to sit down.

"Thanks so much for making this, Sarah. It smells amazing."

"Wait till you taste it, and then tell me then whether it's still amazing," she says, chuckling. "I just eyeballed everything."

"You can eyeball anything you want. You were always a good cook. Definitely a hundred times better than me." I pull up my chair and sit down across from her.

With that, dinner officially begins which is good because I can't talk when I'm enjoying my food, home-cooked, at that. Even the fry bread is still warm and fluffy, the perfect companion to the stew. Still, it's difficult to concentrate on the food when I've got Sarah sitting across from me. Far from the impersonal clinic meeting of this morning, she's even more beautiful, her blue eyes still able to pull me from across any room or in this case, from across the table.

But things have changed between us and we're not exactly friends anymore. We've let secrets destroy what we once had, her secrets and mine.

"So tell me about yourself," Sarah says ten minutes later. "What have you been up to since UNM?"

I tear a piece of fry bread and dip it in the stew. At least she waited until we're finishing up the first round. I suspect I'll probably end up getting a second helping later tonight. "Work, mostly... and I finished my Doctorate six months ago."

"You'll be running for a chapter seat next."

I roll my eyes. "Yeah, right. Let's say my goals don't include running for anything local. I'm happy just doing my own thing."

She wipes the corner of her mouth with a napkin. "I honestly thought you'd be married by now, Benny, with one or two kids."

Sarah's words bring back Noelle and the six years we'd been dating on and off. We'd mostly cooled off when I lived down in Albuquerque studying for my Masters and so I dated a lot of women. Earned myself a nasty reputation but one could say I was busy sowing my oats since I couldn't exactly do that while living on the reservation.

"I'm not thirty yet, Sarah. I'm in no hurry." Or I wasn't until I announced to my family four weeks ago that I'd get back with Noelle and finally ask her to marry me.

"So how come you don't have a girlfriend? Or a side chick, for that matter?"

I wait until I swallow the last of my dinner before answering. "Why so curious?"

Sarah shrugs. "I don't know. You don't look like the type to be unattached."

"I could say that about you, too," I say carefully. "What does your boyfriend think about you working out here in the middle of nowhere?"

"I don't have one," she says, leaning back in her chair. "So what he thinks doesn't matter."

We don't talk for a few minutes, our focus on the food, but I can tell there's something she's not saying.

"What are you doing out here, Sarah?" I ask. "I could have sworn you'd been accepted for a job back in New York before you graduated from UNM. You'd been so happy to have a job lined up so quickly after graduation."

"I decided to give travel nursing a try," she says, picking a crumb from the table and dropping it into her empty bowl.

"Why here?" I ask. "This is so out of the way it's not funny."

"Why not? You said so yourself, Benny. The turnover is high around here. People come in to do their sixteen weeks and leave."

"Is that how long you signed up for?"

She nods. "Yup. I might put in for another round. It's only four hours away from Taos and normally I'd be there on my days off, like tonight."

"Yet you're not. How come?" I push my bowl away from me and rest my forearms on the table. "Surely it's not because you wanted to make me dinner... which happened to be amazing, by the way. Thank you."

"You're welcome." She folds her arms across her chest as she studies me. "You haven't changed, you know. You're still as vain as they come."

"You mistake my confidence for vanity," I say, chuckling. "But forget I asked why you're not with your family–"

"If you really want to know, it's because I don't want

to talk to my dad," she says. "That's why I'm not there tonight. My mom could have let me find out for myself but she called me this morning. Told me he was flying in to spend the next few days with us."

I've been through conversations like this before with Sarah. She has a love-hate relationship with her father, Daniel Drexel, who owns an investment firm in New York. She wants so badly to make him proud of her and when he doesn't tell her the actual words, she's devastated. I couldn't understand it at first—after all, the guy paid for her education, her apartment and her car back in Albuquerque, even a membership at the country club —but when I learned about what happened between Sarah and some married professor she got caught seeing, I kinda got it. It had been a big scandal in Manhattan and so her dad basically sent her away and that's how she ended up at UNM to finish her Nursing degree.

I'd been perfect in his eyes until then, she told me one night when she'd had a lot to drink. That was the thing with Sarah. On the outside she was tough but inside, she was this little girl looking for her father's approval. I was never one to do any armchair psychology but when she asked me to do those things to her that last night she was with me, the same night she strode across the stage to accept her diploma, in the back of my mind, it kinda made sense. But it also didn't.

I'd never done the things she wanted me to do to her that night and I wasn't about to start, not even if we'd end up having the most amazing sex. It was a line I refused to cross and it cost me our friendship.

"Why don't you want to talk to your dad?" I ask, forcing myself back to the present.

"If I tell you, will you promise not to tell anyone?" When I arch an eyebrow in disbelief—like I have time to spread gossip around—she continues. "Let's say I have terrible taste in men. Well, present company not included."

"Thanks, because that would have been a huge blow to my ego if I were."

She glares at me, before sighing. "Anyway, after I left UNM, I went back to New York for a job and I started dating one of the doctors."

"Is that allowed?"

"It's not encouraged but it happens. If anything, we were discreet," she replies.

"Was he married?"

"No. I checked this time. Thirty-two-years-old. Ivy League and all that. No kids. We had fun together and we did some crazy things until one day I realized he just wasn't the one for me." She pauses to play with a loose thread on the place mat in front of her. "When I broke up with him, he didn't take it too well."

"How did he take it?" I ask as Sarah bites her lower lip, her eyes lowering, the picking of the loose thread is her only focus. I lean forward on the table. "How did he take it, Sarah?"

"It started with notes," she says. "Notes on my locker door, the gym, the front door of my apartment."

"What did the notes say?"

"That he missed me and that he'd do anything to get me back," she replies. "When that didn't work, he posted my naked pictures online and the hospital fired me for violating the morality clause."

"Shit, Sarah. That's sick."

She looks at me but not at my eyes, her gaze on something else behind me, maybe my TV or the picture of Tsé Bit'ai'í or Shiprock as it's usually called, hardened magma that was once a part of a volcano and is a highlight to any visit to Northern New Mexico. My sister had taken the picture a few years ago and I liked it so much that I had it enlarged and framed. "He included my address and phone number," she adds in a whisper. "I couldn't answer my phone for weeks. The stuff they said in their messages... they were just vile. And then there were the men who'd wait for me outside my building. Some would make it through the lobby and wait for me by the elevator. I had to call for a restraining order. I had to move." She pauses. "Of course, he denied it all. Claimed that his computer got hacked and that they got into his photo albums or something."

"Yeah, right. Does he know where you are now?" I ask through gritted teeth.

She shakes her head as I look around the apartment. One door, a few windows. Second floor. "I don't think so."

"How many times have you been moving around hoping the pictures don't follow you?"

"This is my third assignment. He found me at the first two but so far, he hasn't found me here," she whispers. "Dad would prefer I didn't work but I can't let Ryan scare me like that."

"Your dad's right. You shouldn't be working. Not out here, Sarah."

Sarah glares at me. "Would you rather I'd have hidden the entire time?"

"Until this thing is resolved, yes," I reply. "Look, I get what you're saying. You don't want him to see you scared, but the thing is, you are."

"No, I'm not," she says. "I get to work and make a difference out here."

I shake my head. Sarah's being her defiant and feisty self and I get it. "I want nothing more than to beat the shit out of this asshole. Ryan's his name?"

She nods, smiling. "Maybe after your arm heals, though. You'll only end up tearing your stitches."

I reach for her hand from across the table. "Sarah, this isn't funny."

"What would you like me to do, Benny? Stay home and hide the whole time like Dad would like me to do? Let this guy scare me from living my life, earning a living? I don't want to be Daddy's girl. I want to earn my own way, make my own money."

"Have you reported this to the police?" I ask. "Has this guy, Ryan, been caught, at least?"

"Of course, I have, but the police can't do anything about it, not if it involves the Internet. They told me I could file a restraining order, which I did, but that doesn't address the pictures released online," she says. "I even tried to take care of things myself. Paid some company to have the pictures removed from a forum but it didn't work. They simply crop up in other forums anyway. It's like playing whack-a-mole. Some guys ended up sharing it because they saved it to their hard drives."

"And your phone number?"

"My dad was paying for that original one because it was under his company plan," she says. "I have a new phone number now. Nothing fancy. Just one of those monthly deals and it's not listed. I call it my burner phone, like they call it on those detective shows."

"You're not exactly working under a burner name," I say. "He can still find out where you're working."

She sighs. "I'm a nurse, Benny. I need a license to work... my real license. I can't just make up some name and expect the company to hire me without a license to back my resume up."

"How long were you and this doctor seeing each other?"

"Eight months," she replies. "We started dating six months after I graduated."

I do the math in my head. Fourteen months after she graduated, she was on her own again but this time she was in trouble. "That's ten months ago." Ten months she's been moving around as a travel nurse because of some guy who can't accept getting dumped.

"Thanks for not asking me why I posed for the pictures," Sarah says softly as I chuckle.

"Well, now that you mentioned it..." I begin as Sarah glares at me and I raise my hands in mock surrender. "Just kidding, Sarah."

"He wanted to take pictures one day and I said sure," she says. "Haven't you ever wanted to have a naked picture of your girlfriend? Something to look at?"

"Not naked, no," I say, pointing to my temple. "That's for up here, but that's just me. I'm also not one to share something special to me. I'm selfish that way."

Sarah looks at me for a few moments, a faint smile on her face. "Whoever's gonna end up with you is gonna be a hell of a lucky woman, Benny. I already envy her."

"I'm not a saint, Sarah. Don't paint me as one."

"No, but you're a man of your word. You stand up for what you believe in," she says, then shrugs. "And when you say no, you mean it. You really mean it."

Ah, she must be referring to that night two years ago. "You're right. I do and I did that night, if that's what you're basing this observation on. Besides, the stuff you asked me to do... I'd expect that between two people with a commitment but we didn't have one in place. We were just friends."

I want to tell her that it would have also cheapened the whole experience. We'd just be two people doing things for the sake of doing them, to try them out all because she was drunk and probably figured I'd be game. But what Sarah wanted required more than just following instructions she found on the Internet. It required a connection between two people and trust that went beyond friendship.

"We were more than just friends, Benny, and you know it even though we never acted on it. That's all we could handle then, I guess," she says, her gaze more direct this time. "It wasn't like you were already sleeping with other women. It wasn't exactly a secret."

"Did you ask this Ryan guy the same things you asked me that night?" I ask, my stomach clenching when Sarah presses her lips together though I don't need to hear her answer.

Of course, she told the guy, and I'm sure he said yes. Probably showed up with fucking bells on.

"Did he do the things you asked him to?" I ask Sarah who begins to bite her cuticles. A few moments later, she lowers her hand.

"That's when he took his pictures, when I couldn't tell him to stop." Her voice emerges as a whisper and I can feel my anger rising as images of Sarah tied up on some bed come to me. *Did he hit her, too? Was she gagged? Was that why she couldn't say no?*

"Is this why you can't come home to talk to your dad? Because this... this fucking animal, Ryan whatever his name is, took pictures of you while you were..." I don't finish what I want to say. I reach for her hands instead and clasp them in mine. This time, tears fill her eyes and it's as if the floor disappears from under me.

Wood scraping against the linoleum floor, I push the chair back, walk around the table and pull Sarah to me. I'm glad she doesn't fight it. Not when it's as if the dam has broken and she utters one sob that tears right through my heart. Holding her in my arms brings everything back —the times spent together laughing and being ourselves, doing our best to remain friends until the night we ended up in my bed and she told me things she regretted hours later. But if Sarah believes her confession ruined everything she and I once had, she's wrong.

For it didn't ruin us, certainly not for me. It made me realize the lie I'd told myself the whole time I was "just" her friend. How I wanted her to be so much more. I wanted her to be my everything. But I never got to tell her that. By the time I went to her apartment the next morning, she was gone.

And now she's broken.

CHAPTER FIVE

Sarah

I DON'T KNOW WHY I HAD TO TELL BENNY everything as if he's still my friend and can be there for me after I ghosted the guy two years earlier. Surely he's got his own life to live and a woman breaking down is the last thing he needs to deal with.

But the moment Benny pulls me into his arms, all my doubts fade away. My fears, too. That's always been the way it was with Benny back then. He wasn't just a friend, he was someone I could trust with my life. It was a connection we had that I destroyed in one night, all because I was too drunk to care about the consequences and then later, too stubborn to stop myself from telling my secrets to someone else who absolutely didn't deserve it.

No wonder Ryan was more than willing to fulfill them. Every single one of them until the day he refused to hear my pleas for him to stop. Stop with the hurting. Stop with the humiliation. Stop with the pictures.

This is just for us, babe. No one else will see this but us.

I feel Benny's hand stroking my hair, his mouth kissing the top of my head as he tells me everything will be alright. But it's his arms that circle me that calm me the most, his deep gravelly voice that vibrates through me. It's his hard body pressing against mine reminding me I'm not alone.

"I want to see what this guy looks like, Sarah," he says. "I want to make sure he doesn't come near you."

I pull away and look at Benny. He's serious, his eyes blazing. He's also angry. "You don't have to, Benny. I'm fine. It's just..."

"It's just what? You'll just keep hiding?" He brushes my tears away with his thumb. "You can't hide forever, Sarah. You can't move from place to place thinking those pictures won't follow you. You'll just be one step ahead but that's not going to solve your problems. Pretty soon, being one step ahead isn't going to be far enough from this man and what he's doing."

I step away from Benny and wipe away the rest of my tears with the back of my hand. Of course, he's right. It's the same thing Dad has been telling me, wanting to sit down and talk to me about a solution even if it means having to tell him everything. But the thought of telling my own father about my kinks makes me cringe, making me not care that it's been over four months since I've seen him, always canceling plans to come home every time I caught whiff of any news that he'd be there, too.

"Come with me tomorrow," Benny says. "I have to drive to Taos for a meeting and come back in two days. We can carpool and I'll drop you off at your parents. If you're not enjoying yourself or want to come back sooner, let me know." When I don't say anything, Benny continues. "Talk to your dad. Have him help you if he can. Get a lawyer, I don't know. You once told me your dad was very well-connected back in New York. I'm sure he'll know a few people."

When I don't say anything, Benny lifts my chin up with his index finger so I'm looking at him. "Fight back, Sarah. Don't run and hide."

"That's easy for you to say. It's not your naked ass all over the Internet."

"Then fight even harder," he says, his eyes darkening. "Don't let this man get the best of you. Talk to your father. Let him help if he wants to. Let me help you. If I have to beat the shit out of this monster, I will."

I pull away. "I brought this on myself, Benny. The things I told you that night... I should have taken the hint when you refused because you said it wasn't right."

"*Then*," Benny says. "It wasn't right *then*, Sarah, not when we were just friends. And no, you didn't bring this to yourself and you need to stop thinking that. That's why you need to stop running as if you asked for this thing to happen because you didn't." He pauses, exhaling. "And stop keeping so many fucking secrets. It's not good for you."

"It's getting late," I say. "I should start clean up and go home."

"No, I do the clean up. That was the deal, remember?" Benny says. "I will follow you home though. I'm not comfortable knowing you'll be driving home alone this late."

"Benny—"

One look from Benny and I know better than to object. Besides, he's right. Come to think of it, I've never left my apartment at night, not since I started my job in Shiprock. I went to work an hour early while there's still light out and went home in the morning, after my morning run. Then I stayed home most of the time, sleeping and waiting for the alarm to sound so I'd hop in the shower and get dressed for work. That's been my life since this nightmare all began. I can't even have coffee with anyone. I'm too scared someone will recognize me from some picture online.

"Think about what I said," Benny says when I walk toward the door and collect my keys from the console table. "I plan on staying two days before heading back."

"What time do you plan on leaving?"

"I usually leave here before seven so I can make it to Taos by ten. Eleven at the latest. My meeting isn't until one in the afternoon but I'd love it if you can ride with me," Benny replies as he opens the front door. "I'll drop you off at your place and you can call me if you want to leave earlier. I usually leave Taos at three to get back here by seven."

"I'll think about it."

Twenty minutes later, I unlock the door to my apartment and Benny follows right behind me. It's not enough for him to simply make sure I walk into the apartment and close the door. He wants to inspect the place and so I let him. I like watching him take over, moving like a big cat through my apartment as he checks the windows to make sure they can't be easily opened from the outside, opens the closets and peers inside.

I don't have a lot of my own stuff in my apartment. It had come furnished, available to the travel nurses who did their sixteen weeks and left and so I didn't need to bring in anything of my own except my clothes. I basically just sleep and eat and watch home movies, secretly anticipating the moment some stranger would tell me that I looked familiar or say something crude like, *I hear you like it rough.*

"Satisfied?" I ask when Benny emerges from the bathroom. Even the tiny bathroom window didn't escape his scrutiny.

"It's good enough," he says, looking around the living room. "Do you know your neighbors?"

"Not really. I mean, we don't hang out or anything," I reply. "But really, Benny, I'm safe here. It's gated and you've got to be buzzed in to enter."

He walks to the door but stops and turns to face me.

"Come with me tomorrow, Sarah. I'll feel better if you do."

"What time do you want to pick me up?"

Benny's grin lights up his face. "Six-thirty. Be prompt."

TRUE TO HIS WORD, Benny arrives at six-thirty with two cups of piñon coffee from a local shop. "I didn't know what you wanted to eat but I figure we can decide on the way there."

"I already had oatmeal." It's a habit I learned from Benny whenever I stayed the night at his place hanging out with him and his friends. We always had oatmeal first thing in the morning. It was the only thing he could make besides coffee. His forte lies in front of the grill. He can make a mean steak.

He chuckles as he takes my backpack and slings it over his shoulder. "Me, too. But we'll stop along the way for something more filling."

We stop at a roadside food stand two hours later. Benny orders a roast mutton sandwich (on fry bread) while I opt for a Navajo taco with homemade pinto beans and ground beef served on fry bread instead of a tortilla.

I'm glad we don't talk about me this time. Instead, we talk about his job. Turns out Benny is based out of Taos since the Bureau of Indian Affairs has an office there.

Sometimes he telecommutes which means he works from anywhere he wants to be or where he's sent to survey or do research. In fact, he'd been out of town the last three weeks or so, checking a waste spill in Utah that never made the news.

"A lot of incidences don't make the news but we do what we can," he says, shrugging. "Right now, I'm finishing up a study I've been doing with the US Army on the effects of uranium mining on Navajo lands. We've been working on the research for the last year and hopefully it can make a difference regarding the policies for my people. But that's something that's beyond my control."

As Benny continues talking, I can see how much he loves what he does, joking that his mother probably loves it more to the point that she invites everyone over whenever he comes home. She usually collects every news clipping that features him and shows it off to anyone who'll listen. It turns a weekend where Benny's planned to fix things around the house into a social event.

"It's like she forgets that she's got three other children," he says, shaking his head. "But I also know she's just really proud of me."

"My mom and my grandmother dote on my younger brother," I say, smiling. "I think it comes with the program."

"Dax, right? How's he doing?" He bites into his mutton sandwich as he waits for my answer.

"He's okay, I guess. Getting ready to graduate from

high school but he hasn't applied to any colleges," I reply. "It's driving my dad crazy especially since Dax has shown no interest in going to college to begin with."

"What about trade school?"

"He's never mentioned it. He just likes hanging out with his friends and playing video games," I reply. "But maybe he'll figure out what he wants to do with his life eventually. Maybe it will take the attention off me."

"You really don't like seeing him, do you?" Benny asks. "Your dad."

I shrug. "It's no biggie. Like you said last night, I need to let him help me if he can."

Seeing Dad may not be high on my list but I miss Nana's cooking and Mom's gentle wisdom. I like watching her throw clay on her wheel, creating something beautiful every time. I wish I had her talents but I don't. Instead, I have Dad's knack for numbers although in my case, it's dosages that I calculate inside my head.

"Thanks for asking me to join you on this drive," I say as Benny takes another bite of his sandwich, his eyes hidden behind dark glasses. The beginnings of a tattoo peek from under the open collar of his white shirt.

"I'm glad you came along," he says after he swallows his food and takes a sip of root beer. "How long do you usually stay with your folks?"

"Two days, although this time, just overnight since I flaked out the first night."

He wipes his mouth with a napkin. "If you need to get back sooner, let me know."

For the next few minutes, we don't talk as I finish my taco. I watch Benny put away the empty paper plates and bowls in the trash, grab two bottles of water from his truck and hand one to me.

"I was just thinking," I begin as Benny sits across from me. "Why didn't you ever call me the last two years?"

"Because you never returned any of my calls and messages after that night," he replies. "I took the hint."

You could have persisted, I almost tell him but I don't. That's Benny for you. He knows a no when he sees one and I certainly gave him a clear no... or as clear as unanswered phone calls and messages can be. Besides, he always had his life, his women. He had Noelle.

"Hey, don't be too hard on yourself, Sarah. What happened between us two years ago is history," he says, opening the passenger door. "Why don't we do this? As of today, we officially start over. What do you say?"

I nod. "That sounds good."

"Let's shake on it," he says, holding out his hand. As I shake his hand, I suddenly feel sheepish. Why the hell are we shaking hands? As if reading my mind, Benny laughs and pulls me to him, wrapping me in a hug.

"Thanks, Benny," I say as I pull away moments later and he touches the tip of my nose with a knuckle.

"Everything will be alright, Sarah. I promise."

We get back on the road and spend the next hour listening to music on the radio as we make our way to Taos. We talk about the three-bedroom, two-bath condo he bought that's close to the Harwood Museum of Art, his roommate, some guy who loves to go rock climbing and often spars with him at the gym, and about his mother and his half-sister Marjorie who live on the reservation in Shiprock, his twin brothers who are just starting high school.

Leaning back in my seat with my feet on the dashboard, it's just like the way we used to be when we'd go on day trips years earlier. Back then, we were just friends.

This time, we're older, and in Benny's case, wiser. We're still friends, but there are things simmering beneath the surface now, planted there by the secret I told him that night two years ago, a confession only one other man knew... the same man who then used it against me, exposing it for the world to see.

Sure, Benny and I can start over right now, erase the things I said that night. But nothing can erase the pictures that have made their way to private chat rooms and forums.

Nothing can erase the shame of what I really am.

CHAPTER SIX

Benny

I park the truck in front of Sarah's childhood home that's behind a walled entrance. It's a pueblo style hacienda with an oversized garage where I see a black Land Rover and a white Mercedes SUV parked in front of its doors. Tall colorful hollyhocks line the front court-yard that leads to a set of double doors that I assume is the entrance into the house. Along one wall, I see herbs growing in a raised bed, parsley, cilantro, and peppers.

"That's a lot of pepper," I say as I turn off the engine. "You guys roast them yourselves?"

"Nana roasts them and makes her own green chile salsa and everything," Sarah says as I push open the front door but she grabs my arm. "I can take it from here, Benny. You don't have to walk me to the front door. Don't you have to prepare for a meeting?"

"It's not for another two hours," I mutter as she reaches for her backpack in the back seat. I hate that she's still panicking at the idea of meeting of her father, but even as I think that, another thought hits me. *Is she embarrassed to be seen with me?* It's not like I haven't met her family before. I met them at her graduation, hours before Sarah showed up at my apartment drunk and determined to get me into bed with a list of things she wanted to try out.

The front door opens as I walk around to her side of the truck and pull open the door. As her parents walk out toward us, Sarah curses under her breath but I squeeze her hand.

"Hey, you'll be fine, Sarah."

"You made it, *mija*. And here I was thinking you weren't coming at all," the woman I met on Sarah's graduation night two years ago says. She's wearing a sleeveless checkered shirt and blue jeans, her forearms streaked with what looks like clay. It's as if she washed her hands but missed washing the clay off her arms.

Sarah pulls her hand away from mine and steps out of the truck, meeting her mother halfway. Pearl Drexel is a stunning woman with jet black hair falling over her shoulders and hazel eyes. Beside her, Daniel Drexel, wearing a blue collared shirt and jeans watches me with narrowed eyes.

"What happened to your car?" he asks as Sarah hugs her mother. "Is anything wrong with it?"

"Benny said he was driving to Taos so I hitched a ride." Sarah kisses her father on the cheek and steps back to stand next to me. "Mom, Dad, you guys remember

Benny, right? From UNM? You met him on graduation night."

Daniel shakes my hand, his grip a little too firm, his eyes never leaving my face. "Of course, I remember. Your friend." The way he says that last word grates at me but I let it go.

Pearl's greeting is a hundred times warmer, hugging me as if I'm an old friend. "Benny Turner! Of course, I remember him, Sarah. Hello, Benny! Do you work out in Shiprock, too?"

"Yes, ma'am. But we have our main office here."

"He's an environmental protection specialist," Sarah says before glancing around. "Where are Dax and Nana?"

"Dax spent the night over at Gabe's and they're probably hanging out at the park," Pearl replies. "Nana is in the kitchen."

"The Bureau of Indian Affairs?" Daniel asks, his expression surprised. "That's who you work for? Their offices are close to the Plaza."

"Yes, sir. Two years now, right after I graduated with my Masters."

"Ah, yes. You were studying for your Masters when we first met," Daniel says, his brow furrowing.

"Yup. Earned my Doctorate last year." I don't even know why I'm telling him about my Doctorate but from the way Daniel's scowl is replaced with a look of surprise, it seems it was necessary to impress him, but only barely. I can almost guess what's going through his mind, that I'm probably no different from the two men his daughter ended up with—just another asshole with a fancy degree fucking his daughter.

"Benny's got a meeting to go to, Dad, so he can't stay long," Sarah says before turning to face me. "Thanks for the ride, Benny. I don't want you to be late."

"You're welcome, Sarah," I say, forcing a smile. "Call me when you're ready to head back. You've got my number, right?"

Sarah nods as I turn to shake Daniel's hand one more time and lean in as Pearl gives me another hug. "You just got here, Benny. You should stay and have something to eat."

"I'm good, thanks, Mrs. Drexel," I say as the front door opens and a gray-haired woman emerges from the house.

"Nana!" Sarah exclaims as she runs toward her, wrapping her in an embrace. A few seconds later, I'm introduced to Sarah's grandmother Anita Anaya whom I'm supposed to call Nana from here on. No exceptions, she insists which is fine with me. Sarah clearly takes after her mother and grandmother when it comes to personality and warmth.

"Have you eaten?" Nana asks and I nod.

"We stopped at a food stand an hour ago," Sarah says as Nana grasps my hand and starts pulling me into the house.

"That means you have room for one of my sausage breakfast burritos then. Do you like green chile, Benny?"

I almost say no but when I catch Daniel's look of annoyance, I tell myself, screw it. Let him guard his turf all he wants. I haven't had homemade green chile in a while. "As a matter of fact, I do, Ma'am... I mean, Nana."

"He just said he ate, Nana," Daniel mutters as Pearl grabs Sarah's arm, pulling her back so they're walking behind Nana and me while Daniel trails behind all of us.

"That's only because you don't want to share, Daniel," Nana says, chuckling as she proceeds to pull me into the house. "Besides, Benny drove Sarah here all the way from Shiprock. He's also a growing boy. *Mira*, Daniel, he's as tall as you."

As the women chuckle at Nana's unabashed appraisal, Daniel does not look amused.

When I leave twenty minutes later, I finally understand why Sarah always told me there was no better cook than her grandmother. One bite of that breakfast burrito —"just a taste," Nana said—and I have to agree. In fact, as I get behind the wheel of my truck, the women saying their goodbyes outside the door as Daniel watches me still unamused, I'm carrying a plastic container with two giant breakfast burritos I know without a doubt I'm ready to guard with my life.

AT THE OFFICE, I do my best to focus on the points I need to touch on at the meeting but it's a struggle. My mother calls and this time I answer the phone. I still have an hour left before the meeting begins.

While I installed two solar panels at the house and bought her a refrigerator and a big-screen TV so my siblings didn't have to be so bored indoors, there's no way I can get a phone line in the area. Mother is probably at the grocery store picking up supplies for the week. It's when she makes all her phone calls and sends her text messages. It's no joke we call cell phones *bil n'joobal* in Navajo which basically means that 'thing you use while spinning around' while searching for a reliable signal.

"Yá'át'ééh, Benny," my mother says in the customary Diné greeting. "I wanted to remind you about next weekend. Do you think you have time to pick up a few things on your way here? Water, too, if you can manage it. A few gallons just in case we run out."

"I will."

"Your granddad might also need your help with some stuff, too," she adds. "The sheep pen needs fixin' and other things."

My grandparents live with my mother and stepfather on the homestead where he and my grandma raised her and her two brothers. It's ancestral land that's at least an hour away from the nearest town if driving my big-ass truck, the bus stop a twenty-minute walk from the front door. It's the world I grew up in after my father died when I was six and my mother decided to return to the reservation and raise me there. It took a lot of getting used to—no electricity or running water—but I got used to it.

"I'll stay the weekend, Shi'ma. Don't worry," I say.

"I know you've been out of town, but I ran into Noelle and her father yesterday and she told me she hasn't heard from you in over a month, not since you two broke up. I didn't even know you broke up again," she says, her tone accusing.

"We cooled off." Same thing.

"I told her that I thought you guys were together since you told us you were going to ask her the big question. Her father's thrilled."

Ah, shit. "Shi'ma, you didn't have to say that. In fact, you didn't have to say anything." That's the thing with extended families. Everyone knows your business.

"The girl can't wait forever, Bidzii," she says, calling me by my Diné name which means strength. "I know marriage is a scary step and you've only been avoiding it like the plague for years, but you two have been together since you danced your first Powwow together."

"I was only a kid then." I also didn't know any better but I did love the rhythm of the drums and the elders' chanting. It was hypnotic. While I haven't danced at any powwow since then, I've watched it every year, usually with Noelle by my side.

"It's been six years since you two went steady. I'm actually glad you two decided to focus on your education in the beginning because with you workin' for the bureau and her involved in that Diné immersion program with the natives, I just know you two can do so much together. You're perfect together, Bidzii," she says as I rest my forehead on my hand and rub my brow. My mother telling Noelle I'm about to pop the question when we're supposed to be broken up makes everything awkward. And if that isn't the biggest hint for Noelle to know that I'm supposed to be getting back with her, I don't know what is. I just wish it were as easy as simply asking her and hearing her say yes.

But that ship sailed the moment I ran into Sarah.

"Shi'ma, I've got a meeting to go to in ten minutes so I can't talk long." A blatant lie since my meeting doesn't start for another half hour, but it's the only thing I can think of. I glance at the clock on the wall. "Why don't I call Noelle right now?"

My mother sighs in relief and after a few more words about next weekend, we say our goodbyes. After I hang up, I realize I've been holding my breath and I let it out, my shoulders relaxing for the first time since I answered her phone call.

It's not like my mother to be pushy but she's got a point. I did say I was going to do something four weeks ago and I haven't done it even if I had to work in Arizona the last three weeks. I could have done it then but I didn't. It doesn't help that everyone but my stepfather was at the house that day and we were all having dinner, my grandparents, my mother and my sister Marjorie at the table with me and my twin brothers on the couch playing a video game. Whether or not I said it then to get them off my back about their endless questions about my love life, it was as good as an official announcement as any.

Alright, I'm going to ask her.

They all looked at me then, their eyes widening. Even my twin half-brothers who stopped playing their game to stare at me in surprise, their game controllers frozen in place between their knees.

For real, bro? Tahoma had said. He's the one with a scar on his forehead from the time he fell off a rock while running up and down a boulder. It's the only way I can tell him and Tsela apart.

Yeah, for real.

Only I never thought I'd run into Sarah Drexel again. I never thought I'd see fear in her eyes for the first time since I've known her. And I never thought I'd still feel the same way I always felt for her back when I first knew her in Albuquerque.

Only this time, there's something else that's made my feelings for her even stronger. It's making my heart race at the thought of her, my belly clenching at the feel of her body against mine. It's everything she told me that night two years that changed everything, adding another layer to the already-complicated dance between us.

I punch Noelle's phone number before I can change my mind and listen to the succession of rings that follow. I hold my breath, hoping she doesn't answer. I let go only when her voicemail picks up and I listen to her voice telling me to leave a message.

But I don't.

I can't.

My throat tightens as I hang up. I blow out a breath and close my eyes. I should be seeing Noelle in my mind. I should be putting her soft voice together with her face but it doesn't happen.

Instead, I see Sarah's face. And in her eyes, I see fear I've never seen there before. I see my cowardice, too, reflected back at me, my desire to fit in and belong, not wanting to straddle two worlds all the time. Just wanting to fit in for once somewhere.

But I know that's impossible. I've done it too long to suddenly not do it. I'd also be lying just as I'm lying to myself now.

I want to belong to my Navajo roots, true, but I also want the love of a woman I cannot have.

CHAPTER SEVEN

Sarah

After Benny leaves, Mom leads me into her workshop while Nana asks Dad to help her with a shelf in the kitchen. It's one of the things that always amazes me about Dad whenever he comes home. He sheds the New York executive and becomes the man about the house, tightening door hinges, fixing crooked shelves, and when the job is too great, hiring the right people for the job instead of struggling with a band saw. But more importantly, he becomes a husband, a father, and a son-in-law.

Sure, he'll disappear into his home office now and then to check on his company's investments, write his emails and send faxes, but he always makes sure that Mom, Nana, or Dax never want for anything when he's home. It's a weird arrangement for my mother but it's worked for them ever since I was eight and Mom, pregnant with Dax, decided New York wasn't for her and returned home to Taos. My grandfather, Luis Teves Anaya, or Papa as I called him, was still alive then and he and Dad expanded the house to accommodate all of us living under one roof. Funny, though, because we could have bought a new house but Mom simply wanted to return home and Nana and Papa were more than happy to welcome her back. As their only child, they wouldn't have wanted any other arrangement.

Meanwhile, Dad still kept the brownstone that we called home back in the Upper East Side and he never really did anything with my bedroom. When I asked him if I could fly back with him so I could return to my old life, my school and my old friends, he refused, saying I had to be with my mother and my future brother. He would have to do the commuting back and forth. A week in New York followed by a week in Taos. Soon, it turned into two weeks in New York and a week in Taos. When Dax was born, he stayed in Taos longer, so awed by my younger brother who was born with lungs of steel you could hear him next door whenever he cried. Now Dax is taller than me and slowly filling out. Spoiled rotten and a Mama's boy, he and I love to tease each other a lot whenever I'm home.

"I made these for you, *mija*. They'll make great bowls for soup or salad for your new place. What do you think?" Mom's voice snaps me out of my thoughts as she hands me two bowls glazed in shades of deep browns, blues, and turquoise.

"Mom, these look amazing. Thanks," I say, studying

them. I love seeing how the glaze dripped on one of the bowls and on the other, the way the spiral developed. Each one is a work of art. I turn them over and grin proudly when I see her signature at the bottom. Pearl Anaya-Drexel.

Legally, Mom doesn't really have a hyphenated last name. She dropped her maiden name when she married Dad and they were both living in New York. But when she moved back to Taos while pregnant with Dax, Dad convinced her to keep her maiden name for her pottery. That way, people would know she was her father's daughter, keeping the tradition alive. These days, Mom holds classes in her home studio and sometimes she goes to schools to teach kids how one can create endless magic with soft clay mixed with water.

She still creates each piece using traditional tools like her father's kick wheel. I remember sitting in her workshop after school with my homework neglected in front of me, too busy watching her stretch soft clay on the wheel with water, shaping it with her slender fingers, her bare foot sending the wheel spinning with a deft kick. When she was done, there was a mug or a bowl or a pitcher, yet to be fired and then glazed. Dax always loved watching her, too, although these days, he prefers hanging out with his friends to staying home.

"One day, these will end up in a museum, Mom," I say, setting the bowls back down on the table. "I'll probably leave them here since I'm only going to be in

Shiprock a few more weeks and I don't want to risk breaking them during the move."

"I'll be happier if people actually use them, *mija*. That's what they're for, to be functional, the same way your Papa preferred them to be," she says, chuckling. "But you're right. It's only a few more weeks and hopefully you can find a job somewhere closer. Have you thought of applying for a job at the hospital here? I'm sure they have openings for you."

"We'll see."

Mom pulls up a chair for me before walking to her glazing kiln and lifting the lid. "So tell me about Benny. How'd you guys end up together?"

"We're not together-together," I say, watching her reach into the kiln to pull out a mug, inspect it, and then set it down on the rack next to her. "He came into my clinic yesterday with an injury."

"Not too bad, I hope?"

"Just a gash on his arm and bump on his head," I reply, shrugging. "But he'll live."

Mom looks up at me expectantly. "And?"

"He mentioned he was heading to Taos today and so... after work I hitched a ride with him." I almost forgot the part about having to fill in for a coworker.

"Oh, that's right. You had to work last night," Mom says. "He looks really good, *mija*. I remember him from your graduation. He was so proud of you he was practically grinning from ear to ear. Do you remember him yelling from the bleachers?"

I laugh. Of course, I remember. I also remember feeling embarrassed as I walked across the stage to get my diploma with him hooting and hollering. And whistling. "Yup. I don't think anyone missed that."

I also remember feeling so nervous that night. I'd made the decision to finally tell Benny my little secret and see if he'd be willing to do them all with me. Well, he didn't. He drove me home instead.

"And then you had a falling out, didn't you?" Mom says. "I remember you stopped talking about him. Like you had a misunderstanding or something."

"Something like that, yeah. But I also got that job in New York, remember? And he got a job, too, so it wasn't like we were going to keep in touch or anything."

"But now you guys are friends again." Mom says as she looks up from her glazing kiln, smiling. "I always wondered what happened to him. I think he's cute. Rugged handsome, if I might say so."

I shrug, doing my best to look like I don't care. "Well, he's alive and kicking."

Mom pulls a mug in blue and gold, turning it in front of her to look for imperfections in the glaze. "You like him."

"No, I don't," I mutter under my breath as Mom sets the mug she's holding on the rack and smiles.

"Yes, you do, *mija*. You always did back when you were both at UNM."

"Well, I don't like him that way and that's that," I say a little too defensively. "Besides, the last time I liked a guy, it didn't work out so well. In fact, make that two men."

"Just because your last boyfriend did what he did doesn't mean every man will do the same," she says. "It says a lot about a man when they set out to hurt a woman like that."

"Anyway, I figure since Dad's here, I should talk to him," I say, getting up. "He should be finished helping Nana, right?"

Mom nods. "Probably. He's been wanting to spend time with you for awhile so I shouldn't be hogging you all to myself."

I leave Mom's studio and make my way to the back yard where Dad has set up the casita in the back as his office. It's a small one-story building that used to be my grandfather's studio space before Dad converted it into a studio apartment complete with its own bathroom and kitchenette. It's separated from the main house by a circular herb garden that Mom and Nana tend together. Rosemary, lavender, and thyme are planted and rotated every few years. When in season, they grow basil, too, and other herbs I'm not familiar with.

I knock on the door and push it open. He's sitting at his desk, typing on his keyboard but he stops when he sees me and beckons for me to sit down.

"Hey, honey, I was just talking to Lionel Chambers. You remember him, right?" he asks as I take a seat across from him. While his office in Manhattan has a view of the Financial District beyond its floor to ceiling windows, the only view he's got in his small converted studio is the garden, the view partially blocked by a tree trunk where as I used to watch squirrels chasing each other to protect their territory. His home office is also more homey than his Manhattan office could ever be, complete with a collection of Mom's bowls on the coffee table by the sofa next to the sliding glass door that leads to another part of the garden.

"The lawyer?" I remember Lionel because he's one of Dad's closest friends. They play golf whenever they can and a few times a week, they meet for drinks at the Metropolitan Club where they talk more business.

"Yes, Lionel Chambers of Chambers, Maynard & Lipman. He has a department that specializes in cases like this, cyberstalking and harassment," Dad says. "But it's going to require your full cooperation. You'll probably need to fly to New York to meet with the lawyers."

"I can arrange that," I say, glad that we're keeping it almost business-like. If there are any questions about the pictures, it means Dad's not the one who'll do the asking. The lawyers will. "What else will he need?"

"Everything you have, records of any communication between you and Ryan. Screenshots of any pictures or new postings that you've seen," he says. "The company security already has your phone and they're recording every call or text message that comes in. All of it will become admissible at some point, but it might take time to fix."

"It's a start, though," I say. "I just wish..."

"It's done, Sarah. There's nothing we can do to undo what happened," Dad says. "Lionel says it will take some time but we have to start somewhere."

He's too calm and I'm not used to it, but at the same time, this is the first time we've talked without arguing in months which means Mom must have talked to him. Probably told him to cool his jets and tread carefully. But a feeling of shame fills me anyway, the realization that this would never have happened if I had the common sense not to pose for pictures in the first place.

"You're not mad at me?"

He leans his forearms on the desk. "Why would I be mad at you, Sarah? Like I said, what's done is done and now we have to work together to deal with this. No more arguing. No more walking away angry all the time, especially when you and I both know we can't undo what happened." He pauses to think for a few moments. "I might need you to stay in town when they finally file the charges against this man which means you'll have to quit work. That way your mother won't be so worried about you all the time. She can't sleep whenever you leave her for Shiprock. Never could, not even when you worked in your last two jobs. She's afraid someone might find out where you live... where you work."

"Dad, I'll be–"

Dad raises his hand to silence me, his eyes narrowing as we hear the slamming of the front door in the main house followed by angry voices. I recognize Dax's voice immediately followed by Gabe Vasquez's voice. He and

Dax are best friends although right now, it doesn't sound like it, not with the angry voices I can hear coming from the house.

Dad gets up from his chair but I beat him to the door and into the main house. I find my brother and his best friend in the living room shoving each other.

"What the hell is going on here?" Dad demands from behind me as Dax turns to face us, his expression quickly shifting from surprise to anger the moment he sees me.

"You! I can't believe you have the nerve to show your face around this town after this... this–" He stops, pulling out a crumpled piece of paper from his jacket pocket and waves it in front of him. "Do you know what this is, Sarah? Do you have any idea?"

From the studio, Mom appears at the door and hurries toward me as Nana emerges from the hallway leading to the bedrooms.

"What the hell happened?" Dad strides across the room and grabs Dax by the shoulders, inspecting his face. "You've got a black eye."

"Him and Larry got into an argument, Uncle Dan," Gabe says. "One minute they were talking and the next, they just started hitting each other."

"You wanna know what he said, Dad?" Dax thrusts the paper into Dad's hand. "Look at this and guess."

"What did he say?" This time it's Mom who asks the question and the men look at her as if just realizing she's in the room. Gabe bites his lower lip and looks away as Dax's expression changes from anger to embarrassment.

Dax hangs his head. "Mom..."

"Answer your mother, Dax," Dad says through gritted teeth.

I watch as my brother's gaze goes from Mom to me, embarrassment giving way to anger. "He said his brother saw pictures of Sarah online. He said it was on a public forum with her name and phone number. He even printed it out in case I didn't believe it," he says, cocking his head toward the paper in Dad's hand. "It's right there. He said you could still see it online. It even has her home address. This address."

"Oh, for fucks' sake," mutters my dad as he glances at my mother who brings her hand to cover her mouth in horror. "Pearl, get her out of here please."

"... and that's when I punched him. No one talks about my sister that way," Dax continues as my mother pulls me into the hallway with Nana.

"Let's go, Sarah," Mom says and I don't object. I don't even have the voice to say anything. Even when I open my mouth, nothing comes out. All I know is that my shame has become my brother's to bear, too.

As Nana tells us she's going to make some chamomile tea for everyone and a compress for Dax's black eye, Mom pulls me in a hug. "*Mija*, it's not your fault."

As Mom's arms tighten around me, I suddenly feel exhausted. I can't get Dax's expression out of my mind. I'd never seen him tremble with rage before, and then there was that look in his eyes, judging me... accusing me.

"It's my fault the moment I agreed to pose for that first picture, Mom," I whisper, fighting back the tears. "I brought this all to myself and now Dax has to deal with it."

It was supposed to be just one picture, an innocent shot of me in his bed. Only there were more pictures that followed and I'd only learn about the video camera later, hidden behind his headboard.

How I thought I could take care of things all by myself is laughable now, especially when my shame followed me all the way home.

CHAPTER EIGHT

Benny

Two hours later, the meeting is over and I spend the rest of the afternoon catching up on paperwork. Unfortunately, all I do is stare at the monitor, not really seeing the words. All I can think about is Sarah and if there's anything I can do to help her besides hunting this Ryan guy down and beating the shit out of him.

By four, I realize it's pointless to keep working, not when I can barely concentrate, and so I gather my things and say goodbye to everyone at the office. I drive to the three-bedroom two-story condo on Kit Carson Road that I bought a year ago with Mariano Payne, an archaeologist who works for the Bureau of Land Management. Given my stints working in Shiprock or wherever else I get sent to by the main office, he pretty much gets full rein of the place but I have no complaints. Mariano's a cool guy, spends most of his time outdoors when he's not working, and is a neat freak like me.

We keep the furnishings minimal. It's a guys' townhouse through and through with a few of the comforts of a Southwestern inspired home. A fireplace, tinwork accents on the walls, and lots of plants that give the place an earthy feel. We could have turned the third bedroom into an entertainment room but we ended up converting it into a home gym instead, complete with a power cage for bench presses, barbell squats and deadlifts, a punching bag, and a treadmill.

When I get home, the first thing I do is place Nana's breakfast burrito in the fridge where Mariano had taped a flyer announcing my favorite band playing at a local bar that night. I can't help but grin. Hanging out with Mariano and the other guys would help distract me from thinking about Sarah. It would also mean a night of dancing two-step with whoever Mariano has invited along.

There's only one problem. If I'm dancing two-step tonight, I want to do it with Sarah. After all, I'd taught her how back when we were students at UNM. She'd been clumsy at first, mostly self-conscious with her movements but she soon got the hang of it. I'm not the best dancer out there but I loved how she followed my lead from the beginning, not insisting to go one way while I went the other.

But I really can't ask Sarah. That would be a date, and I need us to remain friends.

No, I need to do something else.

I need to hit something.

I change into my workout clothes, grab a roll of hand wraps from the shelf and begin wrapping my hand. It's probably too soon to do a round with the bag but I need to do something. After a warm-up of shadow boxing, squats and crunches, I slip on a pair of gloves. The cut in my arm throbs but I ignore it.

Seeing Sarah again has thrown me off my routine. I could barely sleep last night thinking about the last guy she dated, the one who posted her pictures online. She didn't mention it but I'm sure she's aware he posted their videos, too, and while there were only three that I saw after two hours of searching online last night, they were three too many.

Can you keep a secret?

The memory of Sarah's exact words had caught me by surprise. It was her graduation night and I was there, cheering for her. She'd graduated with honors and I was so proud of her, so happy. Probably happier than I should have been as "just" a friend.

When she left to celebrate with her parents, I didn't mind not getting asked to join them. It was a family affair and I was sure I'd celebrate with Sarah another day. And so I hung out with buddies at a bar for a few hours and went home. That's when I found Sarah waiting for me outside my door.

Hands wrapped, gloves on, I start with basic jab, cross, and hook punches. Three minutes. Shit, I should have warmed up first but too late for that now. I take a break, watching the clock on the wall. Thirty seconds.

Why didn't I call her these last two years? Why did I give up so quickly?

Have you ever thought of tying up a woman?

I start again, mixing up my combinations, my breath coming out faster. Hook, cross, hook. Jab, cross, hook, cross. Three minutes. My left arm starts to sting and from the corner of my eye, I spot a small dot of red. Blood. But I don't even care that I've reopened my injury, broken the stitches. I need to hurt. I need to feel pain.

Have you ever thought of dominating a woman? Tying her up? Spanking her?

Sweat drips down my face, stinging my eyes.

What are you trying to tell me, Sarah?

As beads of perspiration continue to roll down my face and neck, I'm glad I invested in foam tiles for my home gym. I'm glad I've got a housekeeper who can mop all that sweat off the floor, disinfect it with whatever she uses.

I don't know who else to ask but I figured I'd ask someone I trusted...

I keep punching the bag, feeling my frustration give way to exhaustion, pain knifing through my arm. I remember Mariano had some type of wound glue in the bathroom. If I have to, I'll have to use that and superglue the crap out of my incision.

Jab, jab, cross. Cross, hook, cross. Jab, cross, jab, hook, hook.

My muscles are screaming now but I don't care. All I can hear is Sarah's voice, see her face as she tells me... no, trusts me with her deepest, darkest secret.

Will you dominate me, Benny? Will you hurt me?

I punch the bag one more time, sweat now mixed with something else. Tears of frustration. Tears of regret.

My breath emerges from my mouth ragged and harsh as I grab the bag, clinging to it as I catch my breath. Sarah's words keep coming, the memories of that night that I've kept locked up inside me finally unleashed and there's no way to stop them.

I want to know how it feels, Benny. I want to know why I can't stop thinking about trying it out with... with you. I trust you.

I let go of the bag, sweat dripping down my lashes, the taste of salt against my lips.

One more hook. One more cross, and this time, I feel a sharp pain in my arm break, the sting that I've been waiting for finally hitting me, reminding me how I fucked up.

Sarah's voice is gone and in its place is just the sound of my breathing, ragged, sharp. A groan escapes my lips as blood drips down my arm and onto the rubber mat, my arm throbbing.

But it's not the cut that Sarah had meticulously stitched closed yesterday that's now opened that hurts the most. No, it's the silence that follows after she asked me those questions... the silence of my refusal just before I drove her home.

MY PHONE RINGS while I'm applying wound glue to the ripped stitches in my arm. Muttering under my breath, I press a hand towel to my arm and hurry to the living room. One glance at the phone display and I grab the phone and press Answer.

"Hey, Sarah. What's up?"

"I know it's late but I was wondering if you'd like to do something tonight. Or we could just hang out."

Cradling the phone on my shoulder, I return to the bathroom and grab a roll of gauze, breaking the seal with my teeth and wrapping it around my arm. "Sure. What did you have in mind?"

"I don't know."

"Hang on." I head to my bedroom and pick out a pair of jeans and a light blue shirt from my closet. Grabbing a pair of boxer briefs, I slip them on. "Guess what. My favorite band's in town. Stateline. Ever heard of them?"

"No, but the name sounds familiar."

"You in the mood to dance two-step with me?"

Sarah doesn't answer for a few moments. "I'm not sure. I don't think it's a good idea for me to be out right now, definitely not around Taos."

I get the hint right away. Something happened. "Sarah, what's going on?"

"One of Dax's friends found my picture online and they got into a fight," she says haltingly.

"Ah, shit. He okay?"

"He got a black eye but he says the other guy had it worse."

I slip one leg into my jeans and then the other. Forget two-step. If she wants to hang out and watch paint dry, then we watch paint dry. "Why don't I come over and pick you up in a few minutes? Just dress casual. We don't even have to go out. We could just hang out here and talk if you want."

"That would be nice."

"I can be there in fifteen... twenty minutes."

I make it to her house in twenty minutes and find her standing outside her front door. There's a black SUV parked in the driveway that wasn't there that afternoon. She's wearing jeans, a long-sleeved shirt over a black top and cowboy boots. As she pulls open the passenger door, I can see that her eyes are puffy.

"How are you feeling?"

"Better now that you're here," she says as she settles herself on the seat and pulls the seat belt across her torso. "I do have to warn you about my curfew. Dad says I need to be home before two or he'll send his security people over to your place."

"You're serious?" I ask as Sarah nods. "Then two it is. Don't want you to turn into a pumpkin or anything."

"Thanks, Benny."

"Have you had dinner?" I ask as I turn the key in the ignition. "We can get something to go–"

"Wait. What happened to your arm?" she asks, her gaze on the hastily wrapped gauze I'd bandaged around my arm. "And what happened to the dressing from yesterday? And is that blood? Did you cut open your stitches?"

I shrug, the wound throbbing now although this time, it has nothing to do with the tetanus shot. I forgot all about that the round with the bag.

"Guess I did."

"Benny, we need to fix that. You're going to get that cut infected," she says, her tone scolding. "We should go to the Emergency Room and have someone stitch it back together."

I shake my head. "No more emergency rooms for me. Not tonight."

"Then I need to get some steri-strip skin closures for that."

"Steri-what?"

Sarah rolls her eyes. "Just get us to a pharmacy, Benny. They'll have what I need so I can fix you."

At the stoplight I turn to look at her. "Did you get to talk to your dad?"

She takes a deep breath and nods. "I'll tell you all about it after I fix you."

Half an hour later, we're back at my condo with a shopping bag full of medical supplies and two dinners-to-go from a nearby restaurant. I'm glad to see Sarah smiling again although the moment we head to the guest bathroom, she's on full nurse mode as she instructs me to stand against the counter. After washing her hands and putting on sterile gloves, she sets to work, first unwrapping the gauze bandage I'd hastily wrapped around my arm and grimacing when she sees the mess I made with the wound glue.

"I can't believe you decided to go for a round with the punching bag. You tore two stitches. Nothing major but still..." She pulls out a bottle of antiseptic from the paper bag, sets it on the counter, and rips the plastic cover off a roll of gauze. "We just need to make sure it doesn't get infected."

"I'll do everything you say from here on, Nurse Sarah."

She glares at me before disinfecting the wound, the sharp sting making me cross-eyed for a moment and she chuckles. "That's what you get for not following instructions the first time."

"Your skills would come in handy during a zombie apocalypse, you know," I murmur when she's almost done closing up the busted stitches using the steri-strips.

"You're not supposed to do anything strenuous, Benny." She wraps the bandage around my arm a lot more securely and neatly than I did earlier. "You could have torn open the whole incision."

"But I didn't," I say. "I've also got you."

Still leaning with my back against the counter, I've been aware of how close she's standing since she started dressing my wound. I've been watching her bite her lower lip as she concentrates on each step that only she knows by rote. Hell, I don't remember anything about first aid right now other than maybe I should get injured more often. Maybe then I'd feel her fingers pressing against my skin, her focus directed solely on me.

But that was minutes ago. As Sarah pulls away to inspect her handiwork now protected under a film of a plastic-like material that she says will allow me to jump in the shower without having to worry about my bandages getting wet, there is nothing else to distract me from her. Right now, there's only her.

"That should do," she says, peeling off her sterile gloves and tossing them in the trash can next to the counter. "I should write down the instructions for you in case you forget. No strenuous activities like boxing or heaven knows what else you decide to do."

"Sex?" I ask as she glares at me. "Just kidding."

"I'm serious, Benny," she says, reaching behind me to gather the wrappers from the counter. "It could have been worse. You could have opened that incision completely and I'd have to take you to the Emergency Room."

As her body brushes across my side, the scent of her hair hitting me in the gut, my stomach clenching, I remind myself to calm the hell down.

Too bad my mouth has other ideas.

"You're a very beautiful woman, Sarah," I murmur as

she steps back and tosses the wrappers in the trash. "Inside and out."

One corner of her mouth curls upward but she eyes me suspiciously. "Yeah. Right."

I bring my hand up, my fingers brushing against her cheek. "I mean it. Don't let anyone make you believe any different," I say as our eyes meet and she holds my gaze. It's only for a split second, the connection I've been waiting for since yesterday morning but as quickly as it comes, it's gone.

"Dinner's getting cold, Benny, and your stomach has been growling for the last ten minutes so I know you're hungry," she says, her voice softening. "But thank you for saying what you just said. It's nice to hear that now and then, especially when I know you mean it."

"Then I should say it more often so you'll believe it."

She pauses, chuckling. "You might have to wait until after dinner to say it again. Priorities."

She's right, of course, because my stomach growls again and after returning all the unused medical supplies to the paper bag and placing it in one of the bathroom cabinets, we head to the dining room. Luckily, the food is still warm and after grabbing two sodas from the fridge, we settle at the table to eat.

The moment I pull the lids off the containers of food we'd ordered, my mouth waters from the aroma of stacked red chile and cheese enchiladas and a large sopapilla stuffed with beans and beef smothered in cheese and green chile that fill the room. What is it about

New Mexican food that I can't get enough of? Besides growing up with it when Dad was still alive, there's nothing like red or green chile to make everything in the world feel right. And from the smile on Sarah's face, I'm guessing she feels the same way.

We set the table and sit down. As we eat, she tells me that she talked to her dad and that it didn't turn out as terrible as she thought it would. It's as if all their defenses were down—hers especially—and they knew that they needed to work together from this moment on. She tells me that her father's best friend owns a law firm in Manhattan. As far as she knew, he specializes in corporate law but her father told her they also have a department that handles cybercrime, harassment... basically, what she's going through. The man can help and Sarah is not saying no. She needs all the help she can get.

As for Dax, he got into a fight with a friend whose older brother found her picture online along with her home address. It's why there was a black SUV parked in front of the house. Even the police might drive by the area to check for non-residents hanging around.

"I never thought it would go this far, Benny, that he'd post my home address. He must have looked up my last name," she says, setting her fork down. "Why would he do that?"

"I don't know but he better pray our paths don't cross," I say.

"Benny, that'll be up to the law."

"That doesn't mean I won't beat the shit out of him if

I run into him, Sarah," I say. "Which reminds me, I need to see what he looks like in case he shows up around Shiprock. He a white boy?"

She nods. "Blond, blue eyes."

"Good. That means he'll stand out."

We hear the sound of a key turning in the lock and Sarah looks at me, her eyes wide, Panicked.

"It's just my roommate, Mariano. He's cool," I say as the front door opens and a tall dark-haired man walks in. He grins when he sees me, setting his backpack on the couch as he makes his way toward the dining table.

"Hey, man, long time no see. It's been, what, six weeks?" he says as we bump fists and I introduce him to Sarah.

"Sarah. From UNM, right? I've heard about you. You're originally from New York, right?" he says as Sarah looks at him in surprise. "You're the runner."

Sarah laughs. "Yes, I am in every sense of the word."

"You guys going to the Pit Stop tonight? I left the flyer on the fridge," Mariano says. "I hope you've got your cowboy boots on tonight, Sarah, because I'm sure this guy right here is gonna sweep you off your feet before the night is over... if he hasn't already."

"Oh, please. We're just friends. Seriously," Sarah says, laughing. "Unfortunately, I wasn't planning on it but–"

"Aw, come on!" Mariano says. "Ever danced two-step before? Country, not the formal stuff."

"Yeah, Benny taught me how back then."

"Then come along with us. You don't have to dance if you don't want to. You can even stick with me if you don't like this guy over here," he says, winking.

"Hey," I protest as Sarah's cheeks turn red, Mariano's enthusiasm clearly working on her but as quickly as she seems happy, her face turns serious as she looks at me.

"Benny, what about...?" she pauses before taking a deep breath and turning to face Mariano. "Alright, I'll go with you guys, although I have a sneaking suspicion your dance card's full already."

"You'd be number three, to be honest," I mutter as Mariano laughs. With two sisters having the hots for him, why pick only one?

As for me, the only woman I want is standing right in front of me, even if she looks unsure. But then, I'd rather live a little instead of spending the entire night talking about some asshole who can't take rejection.

CHAPTER NINE

Sarah

THE PIT STOP IS ALREADY PACKED WHEN BENNY AND I arrive at ten. Mariano had to pick up two friends and so we end up taking separate cars or in this case, trucks but somehow, he gets there before we do. He waves at us from the bar where he's deep in conversation with two gorgeous women.

"They're sisters," Benny says as he guides me toward the bar. "The one on the right is Malia and Carla's the one on the left."

"He's seeing both of them?"

Benny shrugs. "I honestly don't know, but knowing Mariano, I wouldn't put it past him."

"So he's a player?"

"I don't know. I haven't dated him to find out."

I fake-punch Benny as he laughs and drapes his arm over my shoulders, pulling me in a half-hug. After a round of quick introductions, Benny cocks his head toward the bartender. "What do you want to drink?"

"Nothing. I'm fine," I reply, shaking my head. My gaze darts from one stranger to the next as Dax's words this afternoon come back to me. What if someone here saw my picture online, too? What if they recognize me and say something?

As if sensing my apprehension, Benny drapes his arm over my shoulders and pulls me in a side hug. I feel his mouth against my ear. "I'm here, Sarah. I won't let you out of my sight even if it means you might end up dancing with me."

"Is that a threat?" I ask, chuckling as Benny winks at me.

"It's a promise," he says, glancing at the stage where the band is already playing and couples are dancing on the floor. This is a part of Benny no one at UNM ever saw but I guess it's a side of him that he doesn't mind letting out now.

We stay near the bar where Mariano and Benny introduce me to two other friends, men they know through work who had come with their wives. Before long, they leave us to join the couples on the dance floor and Benny nudges my arm. One look at his sheepish grin at wanting to go on the dance floor and I feel all my fear dissolve.

It's been months since I've gone out with friends to have fun, years since I've danced with someone. I let Benny lead me to the dance floor. I take my position as I remember it when he first taught me the two-step. His father had taught him how to dance it, I remember Benny telling me. It was how his parents met, at a bar where some band was playing and she'd gone with her friends after she had an argument with her Navajo boyfriend. He asked her to dance and that was it. His mother fell in love and left the reservation and everything she knew for a man with sparkling blue eyes and a killer smile.

As Benny takes my right arm and positions it to the side at shoulder height, everything he taught me comes back to me. Let him lead. Follow with your right leg because, as he said, women are always right even if I doubt he believes that but it makes it easier to remember to always step with my right.

Quick-quick-slow-slow.

Relax those shoulders.

Don't worry about where he's taking you as you join the rest of the couples dancing counter-clockwise around the dance floor. Just follow and let him lead. Trust him.

Most importantly, let go.

Have fun, Sarah, I tell myself.

Forget the past and just be.

Be here.

"You're thinking too hard again," Benny murmurs when he leads me off the dance floor at the end of the third dance.

"I'm focusing on the steps."

"Focus on me," he says as I look up at him, immediately drawn into his dark eyes that I've avoided all night. "Have I told you how beautiful you are?"

I can feel my cheeks redden beneath his gaze. "Yes, you said it once already."

"That's why I'm saying it again. In case you forgot it already."

"Benny Turner, are you flirting with me?" I laugh as the band strikes up another song and the couples hurry to the dance floor again, us included.

"Always," Benny replies, grinning as we join the couples in the two-step, staying in the middle of the flow while Mariano dances past us with Talia in his arms. He had Carla as his partner during the last dance and I know better than to ask what is really going on with the three of them when the only thing I need to focus on is the man in front of me and the unspoken attraction between us that's been growing with each passing second.

TWO HOURS LATER, my feet are killing me but there's no way I'm stopping. Benny and I must have danced nine out of ten of the songs the band played and by the time he drives me home fifteen minutes before my curfew, I can't stop smiling. I haven't smiled or laughed this much in months that my cheek muscles are hurting.

"Had fun tonight?" Benny parks the truck in front of the house.

"You know I did." I watch him turn off the engine just as raindrops hit the windshield.

He laughs. "Talk about timing." As he reaches for his door handle, I grab his wrist.

"I still have a few minutes. Can we sit for awhile?"

He leans back in his seat. "Sure."

We listen to the rain drum against the roof of the truck, watch the raindrops hit the windshield. Benny takes my hand and brings it to his lips. "I had a wonderful time tonight, Sarah, and I'm glad you enjoyed yourself. You did panic that one time when you thought that guy was staring at you."

"I couldn't stop thinking maybe he saw my picture online and was trying to place me." That's when I missed a step and almost tripped but Benny caught me.

"Come here." Benny tugs my hand and I scoot closer to him on the front seat. The butterflies in my belly come to life the moment I lean my head on his shoulder. His body feels so hot next to mine. The scent of his cologne drives me crazy just like it did when we danced and even more now in such an enclosed space, notes of patchouli, vetiver, and cinnamon blending perfectly with a scent all his own. I want to run my hand over his hard chest and down his flat belly but I remind myself to behave and study his hands instead, tracing the lines on his upturned palm. I just wish Benny did more than just dance with me all night. Take the initiative to do something... anything. I also wish I didn't have a damn curfew, thanks to some guy who handed my brother a printout of his naked sister and now it feels like the whole Drexel household is on lockdown.

The blinking numbers on the digital clock taunt me, like a countdown to the inevitable. "I still can't believe I have a curfew, which means we have ten minutes before I turn into a pumpkin."

Benny grins. "Before this truck turns into a pumpkin, you mean."

"No, before *I* turn into a pumpkin unless you kiss me, Benny," I say it as a joke but it's far from one. I've been wanting Benny to make the first move since he asked me to dance the first time. Then the second and the third. By the fourth dance, I'd given up. The heat of his body emanating from his hands wherever he held me was enough to make me combust on the dance floor. By the seventh dance, I was weak in the knees not because I was tired but because the nearness of him, the way he locked eyes with me when we danced, and the realization that he'd been the one I wanted all this time was too much to bear. Maybe Benny is still seeing Noelle? Or maybe he's got someone else who's got less baggage than I do?

For why hasn't he tried to kiss me yet?

Benny chuckles. "Well, we can't have you turning into a pumpkin now, can we?"

"Don't tease me, Benny. I don't think I can handle any more."

"Then I won't," he murmurs, his face lowering toward mine as his hand cradles my face. I hold my breath, the sensation of his beard on my skin giving me goosebumps. And then there's the kiss that follows, slow and deliberate. Intentional. It starts as a light brush, a whisper—almost a prelude—and then it comes. His mouth covers mine and all I can think of is Benny and the heat between us, growing stronger until it engulfs us leaving nothing but ashes in its wake. As his tongue slips between my lips, his kiss disarms every bit of doubt and fear I've harbored all night. I want to tell him that maybe we should just drive back to his place, retreat into his bedroom and stay there until morning.

His kiss grows deeper and I rest my hand on his shoulder before letting it slide down his hard chest. There's no denying that I want him just as much as I wanted him two years ago, if not more. Back then I'd sworn off men so that could focus on finishing the degree that had been cut short in New York because of a man— the married professor—and I sure as heck wasn't going to let that happen again, not even with Benny. At least, not until I graduated with honors, showing my father that I could achieve something if I put my mind to it.

That's when I thought I could finally focus on Benny. After all, we'd flirted the whole time we knew each other and finally, I could touch him the way I'd always dreamed of touching him even if we were both going our separate ways in the next few days. I was also drunk, suddenly determined to ask him if he was willing to try something new with me. So flippant, too confident. Too drunk. No wonder the man balked.

"You okay?" Benny asks as he studies my face. "You disappeared on me."

"I was just remembering the last time we did this. It didn't work out too well. I don't want complications this time."

"No more complications. Besides, you were drunk then... but you're not drunk now," he says. "Does this make you uncomfortable?"

I shake my head. "Only if I think about that night."

"Then don't think about it. Be here... with me." He lowers his face again and this time, I heed his advice. I take in the manly scent of his skin and the minty taste of his tongue on mine. I lose myself to the sensations that overthrow all reason, my hand drifting lower to the buckle of his jeans until Benny wraps his hand on my wrist, stopping me from going lower.

"Not yet, *nizhoni*," he murmurs as as the porch light turns on and I jump away from Benny.

"Oh great! Is it two already?" I mutter as the front door opens and my father steps out and peers at the truck.

"Two o'clock, on the dot," Benny says as I straighten my blouse.

"Can you believe this? I'm twenty-six-years-old, for crying out loud. I'm too old for curfews."

"But not too old to have a father worrying about you, Sarah," Benny says as Mom pops her head out from behind Dad's shoulder. "Or a mother."

I brush my hair with my fingers. Clothes I can fix,

same with hair. But I'm still blushing and there's nothing I can do about that. "They should be asleep."

"And you should be inside," Benny says, reaching for an umbrella from the back seat. "Hold up and let me open the door for you."

He gets out of the truck and opens the umbrella as he walks around the truck, holding it up for me as I push open the door. With the rain coming down hard, the umbrella is useless but he uses it anyway, laughing as we run toward the house.

"Mr. Drexel. Mrs. Drexel," Benny says, closing the umbrella and shaking off the water on the side of the porch. "Sorry we're late."

My dad makes a show of glancing at his watch. "One minute."

"That's not too bad, is it, love?" Mom asks, stifling a yawn. She's got a blanket wrapped over her shoulders.

"You guys shouldn't have stayed up," I say.

"We just finished a re-watch of *African Queen*. It's our favorite," Mom says. "Have you seen it, Benny?"

"The one with Katherine Hepburn and Humphrey Bogart?" Benny asks. "Yeah, I have. It was one of my dad's favorites."

"Well, thank you for driving her home, Benny," Dad says stiffly. "We can discuss movies another time, preferably during the day."

"Dad," I say, shaking my head. Why does he have to be such a party pooper?

"Why don't you come in, Benny?" Mom asks and Benny shakes his head.

"I should get going," he says before turning to face me. "Good night, Sarah. Call me when you're ready to head back tomorrow."

"Three work for you?" I ask and he nods. "Thanks, Benny. I had a lot of fun tonight."

He moves in to give me a kiss but stops himself and runs back to the truck. The three of us watch him drive away before Dad ushers us inside and I see Dax in his pajamas asleep on the loveseat, his legs draped over the armrest. At seventeen, he's outgrown the phase where he was all arms and legs and is now filling out.

"You guys didn't have to wait up for me," I say as I switch off the TV that still has the credits for *The African Queen* paused on the screen.

"We weren't," Dad says. "It's movie night. Dax gets to pick his action flick and then your mom and I get to choose a classic. Always guaranteed to put your brother to sleep in no time."

"How's his eye?"

"Nana put arnica on it so it shouldn't look so bad," Mom replies, nudging Dax gently. "*Mijo*, wake up. Your sister's home."

Dax sits up, his thick dark hair sticking out in places. As he rubs his good eye, he looks at me and yawns. "About time you got home."

"So you weren't waiting up for me," I say, shaking my head as I look at the three of them. "Right."

"We've got security people now," Dax says, pointing to a corner of the living room. "And cameras, too. High-tech stuff."

I turn to face Dad. "Is this all necessary?"

"Your ex-boyfriend posted our address online with your picture, Sarah. Of course, it's necessary," he replies. "Police are going to beef up their patrols in the neighborhood to make sure there are no strangers hanging around and there'll be two security guys staying here when I leave and it'll be just your mom and Nana here at home. The last thing I need is having strangers thinking they can do whatever they want with my family."

The gravity of the situation hits me like a punch in the gut and I can't believe I brought this on my family. My mother, my brother. Nana.

A sob escapes my throat but no words make it out of my mouth, only a wail of frustration and shame as Mom crosses the distance between us and wraps her arms around me.

"It's okay, *mija*. Your dad's got everything set up and we'll be okay. We'll take care of this together... as a family." As she strokes my hair, I take in the scent of lavender on her skin and the earthy scent of clay that must have clung to her clothes after hours spent in her studio.

In her arms, I'm a child of eight again, confused at the change of scenery and blaming her for everything, for wanting to come live in this small town where nothing happened and where her usual routine of hanging out with her friends at the country club and running the

PTA meetings were now replaced with hours spent at her father's pottery studio, barefoot in front of his kick wheel, her hands and arms covered in dried clay as she relearned everything she used to know before she moved to New York for college and met Dad.

It didn't matter to me how I'd never seen her so happy before that moment. What mattered was that I wasn't in New York anymore and how dare my father not allow me to stay with him. Underneath all the anger, I'd convinced myself I must have done something wrong. For why wasn't I Daddy's girl anymore, the one who could do and get everything she wanted?

And maybe that's why I did all the crazy things I could think of just to get Dad to come home and notice me. Maybe he'd tire of hearing about all my antics that he'd take me away from Taos and move me back to New York again where I could be with all my old friends. I even tried flunking school thinking if I did, they'd send me back to New York and out of Mom's hair. I didn't even show up for the summer makeup classes that would have guaranteed a passing grade. But even that plan backfired on me. That's what happens when you fool yourself into believing you can pressure your parents— your father especially—to give you everything you want. You learn the hard way and you repeat 8th grade even though you were a straight-A student.

And maybe that's why I always pushed the envelope from then on. Even my relationship with the professor in New York was pushing it. I knew it the moment Dad ran into us at Da Marino's where I'd taken Marc, showing off to him that this was one of the places my Dad hung out and where I went to when I felt like it. All it took was one look and Dad didn't need to ask me how old Marc was. The difference was three years.

Is he married? Dad had asked.

He's separated.

Is he married? He'd asked again, through gritted teeth this time. *Yes or no, Sarah.*

Yes, but he's filing for divorce.

Two weeks later, Marc's wife would be waiting for us in the lobby of the hotel where Marc and I had spent the weekend. She made sure to bring the kids with her, as if to remind him that not only was he still very married, they had children together—three little girls with ringlets in their blonde hair. Five-year-old twins and a three-year-old with a cochlear implant.

After the scandal broke, Dad sent me packing to Albuquerque where I told myself not to get involved with men ever again, not until after I graduated with honors and prove to him that I wasn't the sex-starved woman people in New York—his friends and colleagues, most likely—painted me out to be. Only it didn't take too long before I'd fail Dad again when I returned to New York after my graduation. That's when I started seeing Ryan Thayer, one of the young doctors in my department who I thought was perfect in every way. He even indulged me the same things Benny refused me that night—a bit of BDSM here and there, nothing serious.

But I should have known that no one could ever be that perfect. When Ryan proved to be too controlling and too possessive, I broke up with him and that's when I found out just how far he'd go to get me back, stalking me even after I moved away. When he realized I wasn't coming back, that's when he decided to make my life miserable, posting my pictures along with my personal information online.

Only now he's taking it one step further.

As if making my life miserable wasn't enough, now he's determined to make my family's life miserable as well.

CHAPTER TEN

Benny

THE TOWNHOUSE IS EMPTY WHEN I ARRIVE HOME. Mariano must have opted to stay at the sisters' condo tonight and I'm glad. I need to be alone with my thoughts even though thinking is the last thing I want to do. I've been thinking enough as it is. After kissing Sarah, I need a cold shower and I need it now.

In my bathroom, I step into the shower stall and twist the knob to a blast of icy water, wincing as the water hits my skin. It's a sobering sensation, a harsh reminder that I can't risk falling for Sarah. She's way out of my league. She belongs to a world so far from my own. There's also that promise that I now need to keep even if it means ignoring everything else.

But the cold doesn't do anything to ease the tension in my muscles. It does nothing to tame the desire raging inside me for the woman I can't have.

Love was never meant to be in my vocabulary, not

when duty trumped everything else. I'm not just the first one in my extended family to earn a college degree—and a doctorate at that—I'm the one who has the means to support them, from my mother whose husband spends all his money on booze off the reservation every weekend that I don't see how he can keep his job at the power plant for long to my sister with her apartment near the college and her car. And then there are my twin brothers' savings plans that I've set up should they decide to go to college and need to pay for living expenses.

Duty. That's what I was raised to do, to provide for my family when I can, the same way my late father provided me with the trust fund that paid for everything I needed while attending college. It afforded me a way out of the reservation so I could come back and help as many as I could. It's just the way it is and there's no way I'm bucking that trend... or breaking the promise I made about getting back with Noelle and finally getting married.

But it's not Noelle who's been in my mind for the last two days. Instead, every second has been filled with the scent, the feel, and the need of holding another woman in my arms, a woman I know I can't have. To have Sarah would be abandoning my duty to my family and my clan, as a Diné. I used to joke to Sarah back in Albuquerque that I was spoken for back home. That's why I played when I could. But I'm not playing now. I can't.

My erection is as hard as ever, my cock begging for release. My hand moves down my body, my fingers dancing across my shaft. I gasp, the vision of Sarah's hands wrapping around me, stroking me. Pinpricks travel up and down my spine, my hand squeezing once, twice, before I let go, the water turning warm now, hitting my back. I turn the dial again and for the second time, icy cold water hits me though it does nothing to quench the fire that's been raging through my body all the way to my cock. An ache that I've been fighting for so long.

I blow a long breath through my mouth, closing my eyes as I will myself to remember the promise I made to my family, to our clans. It's the same promise I made to myself so long ago, in the midst of one of my stepfather's beatings when I forgot to do something he'd ordered me to do. I was going to prove him wrong. I was going to be as good a Diné as I was raised to be. And even better, I'd provide—for everyone, even if part of it was done out of spite for everything he put me through before my grandfather took me under his wing.

The water shifts to warm again, my heartbeat back to normal as I lean my hands on the wall in front of me, letting the water wash over my back, over the scars my stepfather left behind, from the whips and the cigarettes he used to smoke. Duty. It'll always be about duty. Proving myself until there'll be nothing left to prove.

AFTER SPENDING the morning sorting through all the mail I'd received while I was gone, I arrive at the

Drexels' at three in the afternoon. I shouldn't be nervous, but I am, as if I'm meeting her parents for the first time. Forget that I've already met them twice or that last night, I swore to remember my duty and the promise I made.

As I step out of the truck, Sarah's brother Dax appears from the side of the house. The skin under his eye is swollen and there's a faint tinge of yellow. The black eye.

"Nice truck," he says, his hands in his jeans pockets. "So you dating my sister or what?"

"I'm a friend." I could laugh at such an ambitious declaration. My feelings for Sarah have been far from platonic since that damn kiss.

"You don't look at her like you're a friend," Dax says, peering at me. He's already got that cocky air about him and right now, he's doing his best to act like an alpha, needing to protect his turf. In this case, his sister. After what Sarah told me last night about him getting into a fight to protect her reputation, I get it. But that doesn't mean I'm going to let an seventeen-year-old tell me how I'm supposed to act around his sister.

"How do I look at her?"

"Like you want to get into her pants. That's true, isn't it?" Dax squares his shoulders back, his chest puffing. "Just letting you know, dude, you hurt her, you're gonna hear from me."

I try not to grin. I remember saying the exact same thing when Marjorie had some guy coming by the house years earlier. He happened to stop by when I was visiting and I made sure he'd never forget that Marjorie had an older brother. "I'll remember that."

"You better." As Dax balls his fists at his sides, I can see the defined muscles of his forearms and his bruised knuckles.

"You work out." It's not a question but a statement and it seems to catch Dax off-guard. He follows my gaze and brings his hand in front of his face, opening and closing his fist.

"Yeah, I do. Dad set up a home gym for me in the back," he says, his gaze returning to me, assessing me. "Looks like you do, too."

"You box?"

He shakes his head. "Not yet. You?"

"Got a bag at home but I go to Taos Boxing Center whenever I can. You heard of them?"

He thinks for a moment, his defensiveness gone. "Sounds familiar."

"You should give it a try. I have a feeling you'd be good at it," I say as the front door opens and Sarah emerges with her backpack. Her dark hair falls loosely over her shoulders and the pink top she wears accentuates everything I love about her. Feminine, sexy, with a smile that can light up a dark day.

"Hey, Benny. Hey, bro." She looks at me and then her brother, her brow furrowing. "What are you guys talking about?"

"Guy stuff," Dax replies as his scowl returns but I

don't say anything. The guy loves his sister and that's fine with me.

Taking Sarah's backpack, I open the passenger door and set it in the back seat. "You ready?"

"Nana is still packing food for us," Sarah replies before turning to face Dax. "Hey, you okay?"

"I'm cool," he replies as Sarah wraps her arms around him as he tries to walk away but he's not really trying too hard. He grins when Sarah pinches his cheek.

"It's all going to work out, okay?" She says as she steps away. "You make sure to put that arnica gel around your eye so the skin doesn't turn purple."

"I will," he mutters almost sheepishly. "Anyway, I'm going back inside to help Nana."

When Dax returns into the house, I lean against the truck. "He's very protective of you."

Sarah chuckles. "Well, he was pissed at me yesterday, but you're right. He is protective of me, just as I am of him. I mean, this address is out there for the world to see." She stops when a police car drives past the gate and she waves.

"What a fucking asshole."

She shrugs. "Dad had security cameras installed and the police are going to be patrolling the area for awhile. We also have security guys staying in the back house now. They'll be here when Dad leaves."

I can see her mood turn dark and I take her hand, squeezing it. "Things will work out, Sarah. This guy will pay for what he's doing to you."

"Easier said than done, but it's a start. I'll also need to fly to New York one of these days to build the case against him which means I'll have to relive everything," she says, sighing. "My idea of a fun time."

"I can come with you if you want."

She smiles. "Thanks, Benny, but that's okay. My dad will be there."

"Just know I'm a phone call away."

Sarah laughs. "Yeah, right, and New York is just a hop, skip and a jump from here."

I pinch her chin playfully. "For you, Sarah, I'd do more than hop, skip, and jump."

She eyes me, looking unconvinced. "Really?"

"Yup, I would."

"That's a nice thought, but I'm serious. I've got my dad. He'll be in New York then. That's why the security guys will be in the house with Mom, Nana, and Dax. He's gonna be in New York for at least four... five weeks this time. They're moving to a new office. Bigger."

"I can't imagine how he can leave your mother for weeks at a time. I'd go crazy."

Sarah shrugs. "It's how they seem to work the best, I guess. Mom hates New York and it's how Dad is able to afford all this." She waves her hand toward house behind her. "You could say they're trade-offs."

"I guess I'm different," I say as Sarah meets my gaze, our first kiss last night coming back to me, the feel of her lips, the taste of her tongue. "I want my woman with me all the time. I wouldn't be able to be away from her for a week, much less two."

"Your woman. I like the sound of that." Sarah bites her lower lip as she studies me. "Sounds like you're staking a claim or something." Behind her, the front door opens and her parents, Dax, and Nana step outside.

"I am," I growl as Sarah steps back, blushing.

"I made you these, *mija*." Nana hands a pile of plastic containers to Sarah. "And these are for you, Benny," she adds as Dax steps forward and thrusts a plastic container toward me.

"Blue corn enchiladas. Red chiles, cheese and onions," Nana says. "I'd have topped it with a fried egg but since you guys are on your way back, maybe you can do it when you're ready to eat."

"Blue corn enchiladas?" I look at the container, my mouth watering. "Well, in that case, Nana, thank you. I can't wait to try it."

I open the truck door and arrange the plastic containers behind the front passenger seat before turning to face the Drexel family again. Sarah's busy hugging everyone goodbye and promising to be back in a week or two while I shake hands with Dax who's still not sure what to think about me. When I shake Daniel's hand, I can see from the way his jaw clenches that he's still not impressed with me either. But if he wanted to relay his sentiments in words, Pearl doesn't give him a chance for she and Nana step toward me and Daniel makes way for them.

"You drive safe, okay? We hope to see you again soon, Benny," Pearl wraps me in a hug followed by Nana. As the older woman strokes my bearded cheek, Pearl says something in Spanish that makes Sarah blush and Daniel scowl even more.

In the truck as we drive off, I ask Sarah what her mother said and she blushes even more. At first, she resists.

"I can't tell you, Benny. It's something between women."

"Your dad heard it," I say, grinning. "He didn't look too happy."

Sarah chuckles, her cheeks reddening. "She says you're a keeper and that I shouldn't let you go."

The heat that rises to my face is something that catches me by surprise. The urge to turn around and give Pearl Drexel a hug is another, but I force myself to remain calm. Duty, I tell myself again and again, like a mantra. Still, it doesn't stop me from being curious. "What do you think?"

Sarah bites her lip and winks at me. "My mother's hardly ever wrong."

FOR THE NEXT THREE HOURS, I do my best to stay within the legal speed limit while ignoring the undercurrent of anticipation between us. It's there and it's thick, filling the spaces between our words and our glances.

Sure, we talk about stuff like who's singing the current song on the radio or if my AC/DC CD is the same one from our UNM days, but that's only to pass the time, a distraction for what's really going on. The stolen glances and the knowing looks we exchange throughout the drive tell me all I need to know about where we're going to end up if we don't stop.

Why did I have to kiss her last night? And why am I feeling thrilled learning her mother considers me a keeper? Noelle probably thought the same thing and look what that got her. Six years of waiting for her on-again-off-again boyfriend to make up his mind, the same on-again-off-again boyfriend who's now thinking of sleeping with someone else.

"Are you okay?" Sarah asks as I slow down and exit the highway. "You've rarely said anything the past two hours."

"We talked about music."

"Yeah, but you've been mostly quiet outside of that."

I shrug. "Just thinking about work in the morning, that's all."

Sarah doesn't say anything for a few minutes, her eyes on the road.

"I'm sorry my mom said what she said," she says when I stop at a light. "It's not like we're dating or anything."

I shrug. "It's no big deal."

"It is when you close up on me like you just did."

I exhale, grateful that the light turns green which means I'll be dropping her off at her apartment in no time. "I'm really just thinking about work, Sarah. That's all."

She doesn't say anything for the rest of the drive back to her apartment, the invisible wall between us turning the atmosphere in the cab almost stifling. As soon as I stop the truck in front of her apartment, Sarah unclips her seatbelt and grabs her backpack from the back of my seat.

"Thanks so much for the ride, Benny," she says, refusing to meet my eyes as she pulls open the door and jumps out.

"Sarah, wait up." I do my best to keep my voice calm, grabbing the bag of food at the back of the cab and following her to her front door.

"What are you doing?" She stops in front of her apartment building and faces me. "You should be heading home. It's late and I don't want to interfere with your work any further."

"I'm going to walk you to your apartment and check every nook and cranny before I leave," I reply as she punches a code on the panel next to the door.

"I'm not a damsel in distress, Benny," she says as she pulls open the door and walks in. "I can take care of myself."

"Will you let me check, at least?"

"And then what? You'll fight the intruder yourself?

Or call 911?" She presses a button for the elevator and the doors slide open. I follow her inside. "Go live your life, Benny. Don't lead me on."

"Then I won't," I say, the hurt in her eyes making my chest tighten. "I'll leave as soon as I make sure your apartment is safe."

"Whatever makes you feel good about yourself, Benny," Sarah says as the elevator doors slide open and we step out. As she unlocks the door to her apartment, I know it's for the best. Last night was a mistake and I can't make it worse by following what my heart really wants. I'll only hurt Sarah and that's the last thing I want to do.

CHAPTER ELEVEN

Sarah

I'M PISSED. I'M DISAPPOINTED. AND I'M HORNY AS hell. Too bad Benny suddenly isn't about to give in one inch.

Well, I'm going to show him that I couldn't care less about him. I don't need him and I don't want him in my life. Not anymore. What the hell was I thinking last night, believing he and I actually had something... a spark, at least? Because there was a spark—a damn fire, even—on that dance floor last night.

And then there was his kiss.

How the hell can he tease me with a kiss and then a few hours later, back off like he'd just realized he'd kissed a leper? Has he seen my pictures online? Has he decided I'm suddenly not good enough?

I watch Benny walk across my living room, checking the windows as thunder rumbles in the distance. He disappears in my bathroom and then my bedroom. I can't believe I let him in, trusted him? I can't believe how gullible I've been.

Crossing my arms in front of me, I stand by my door. I should be grateful that he's taking the time to check but I'm not. By the time he walks out into the living room and announces that everything looks fine, I'm livid. Fine, my ass.

"Get out and never talk to me again."

Benny's jaw clenches and he nods, not saying a word. My heart sinks. Why isn't he saying something... anything? After the last two days... after all the flirting, why is he suddenly closed up?

"Is that it?" I ask angrily as he brushes past me and reaches for the doorknob. "You're just going to walk away like that? After last night... after... after kissing me and making me believe–"

"Make you believe what?"

I look up, aware that he's standing so close to me. His eyes are blazing, the heat from his body unmistakable. It sears right through me. But I don't let it affect me. I can't.

"Make me believe there's more to us than just friends," I reply, my heart racing.

"Because we are friends, Sarah," he says.

"Then why did you kiss me last night?" When he doesn't answer, I continue. "Look, if you had no intention for that kiss to go anywhere, you shouldn't have done it. You shouldn't have led me on. You should have just said no like you did that first time two years ago. But no, you had to kiss me last night. And for whatever reason you did it, guess what? It worked! You made me expect something that you never meant to happen. You made me—"

I don't finish what I say for Benny suddenly presses me against the wall, his hands cupping my face, his knee wedged between my thighs as his mouth descends on mine. The kiss is angry, deep, primal, his tongue sweeping across my upper lip before plunging deep in my mouth, tasting me, claiming me. I wrap my arms around his neck, pulling him closer, my nipples hardening against his chest. I don't care what he thinks anymore. I don't care. I don't care.

I. Don't. Care.

All I care about is this moment, Benny staking his claim on me as one hand leaves my face to move down my neck and lower, cupping my breast and squeezing it. I moan against his mouth, aware that my body is on fire under his touch, his thumb circling around a taut nipple through my lace bra.

He pulls away, his eyes dark with desire, his nostrils flaring. "You talk too much. Do you know that?"

"No, I didn't, but I couldn't let you just walk away like that without letting you know how I feel."

He groans. "I've never wanted anyone as bad as I've wanted you, Sarah. Since the beginning..."

"Then show me," I breathe as Benny lowers his face again, this time kissing my neck, his teeth grazing my skin, his tongue blazing a trail along the sensitive skin behind my ear, making me shiver with anticipation. I moan at the possessiveness of it all, as if two long years spent apart ends at this moment when there are no more walls, no more excuses why we can't do this.

No more fear.

I work the buttons of his shirt, desperate to feel my hands against his hot taut skin but Benny grabs my wrists and brings them above my head, trapping me with his strong hands. I don't fight him. His grip is tight but not painful. It's possessive and powerful, just the way I like it. His mouth leaves my neck to claim my mouth again. Tasting, owning, possessing.

Heat pools between my legs as my knees threaten to fold under me. He slides a hand down my shirt, unbuttoning it. I moan, kissing him back, my tongue slipping between his teeth. There's nothing gentle about this and I like it. I crave it. I'm ready to lose myself to him as he rubs his thumb against the lace of my bra, teasing my nipple. As he rubs his hips against mine, the feel of his erection is unmistakable.

Suddenly Benny pulls away and my heart sinks. "What's wrong?" I ask as he lets go of my wrists. I don't think I can take any more.

"Your bedroom, or I'm going to take you right here," he rasps and I grab his wrist, guiding him down the hallway leading to my bedroom, my heart hammering inside my chest. It's happening. It's really happening. Benny in my apartment, in my bedroom. And this time, he's not saying, *no, not tonight, Sarah,* like he did that night two years ago. Sure, I'd been drunk then, all my inhibitions gone as I dared to tell my best friend my deepest darkest secrets believing he'd go for it. After all, he had a crush on me, didn't he? So why the hell wouldn't he?

Only he didn't, not then.

When we reach my bedroom, we stop in front of my bed and I feel Benny's arms circle my waist from behind, nuzzling his face into my neck. His beard scratches my skin as he kisses me, blazing a whisper of a trail from my shoulder up to the skin behind my ear. Goosebumps erupt on my skin as I bring my head back, his tongue soft and hot against my skin.

"Undo your jeans, Sarah," he murmurs and I do as he orders, my head resting against his shoulder, his fingers drawing maddening circles around my nipple through my lace bra. His breath is warm against my skin, searing through every part of me that he touches with his mouth, his tongue, his fingers. I bring one arm down, my hand reaching for him, my other arm looping over his head, resting on the back of his neck. I want more. No, I want it all. When Benny slides his hand inside my jeans, I moan, arching my back.

"Stay still, Sarah, or I'll stop."

My breath hitches at the sound of his voice growling into my ear. It's different now. Commanding, claiming, owning. My heart races. I do as he says. I stay still, waiting for him to make the next move.

His hand moves up to my breasts again, joining the other in squeezing my breasts and pulling my nipples through the lace. They're hard as pebbles between his fingers and I shudder as his mouth finds the skin behind my ear and he sucks on it softly. My belly clenches. I want it all right now but I know better than to insist on it.

Benny's hands move away from my breasts and slide behind me to undo the hooks of my bra. His fingers graze the skin under my arm, his hand gently guiding my arm down as the strap of my bra slides off my shoulders. He turns me around, his mouth meeting mine now although this time, he takes his time, his tongue slipping across my lower lip, grazing across my upper lip. Teasing me. Taunting me.

"Benny... please."

"Get on the bed," he murmurs against my mouth and as I do so, lying on my back on the middle of the bed, he undoes the rest of the buttons of his shirt, shrugging it off his shoulders. My mouth turns dry. Tribal tattoos cover his right chest, traveling all the way down his arm. Another set of tattoos graces his left forearm. Tanned skin, short curly hairs along his chest narrowing down the center of his torso to his jeans, Benny is breathtaking. He never used to have those tattoos when I knew him at UNM but as I study them in the semi-darkness, it's as if he'd always had them. They fit him even if the designs look nothing like what I'd associate as Navajo. But at the same time, what the hell do I know about that? Besides, I've got better things to think about... like the moment Benny pulls down his jeans and I see his cock, so big and beautiful, pre-cum glistening along the tip.

He gets on the bed and reaches for the waistband of my panties. Lifting my hips to help him, Benny slides my panties down my hip. He tosses it on the heap of our clothes at the foot of the bed and kneels back to look at me.

"Do you like what you see?" I ask and one side of his mouth lifts in a smile.

"Why don't I show you just how much I love it?" He replies and I don't protest when he spreads my legs, kissing the skin on the inside of my thigh beginning just above the knee, one and then the other. His beard scratches my skin. His mouth inflames every piece of me that he kisses, that trail from the inside of my knee up my thigh and higher, between my legs. When I feel his hot breath there, I hold my breath, my heart racing, blood rushing through my temples.

Never in a million years did I think this moment would ever happen between us, him in my bed, all mine.

"You're so beautiful. Ethereal. Perfect," Benny murmurs and my heart soars, my breath catching when his mouth grazes my folds, his hot tongue tasting me. I close my eyes, savoring the sensations that hit me, the feel of his arms around my thighs holding me down, one hand pressing my belly down as he pulls me toward him possessive and demanding. From this moment on, I'm his, all his and there will never be anyone else.

The feeling of his mouth and tongue on my folds is dizzying. It's a torment that has me gritting my teeth as I feel my orgasm building and building. He finds my sensitive nub and sucks. I muffle my scream with my hand, my knees moving toward my chest, opening myself up to him even more. He sucks again and I know I'm there, so close... until I am. I come hard, bucking my hips against him as his arms hold my hips down, pinning me in place. I feel myself shuddering, trembling under his touch, vibrating with an energy I've never felt before. It's euphoric.

"Benny, fuck me," I whisper hoarsely when he lifts his head from between my legs. I'm lost in a haze of emotions, my body humming with its release but needing more, craving him inside me.

The bed shift as he moves away and when it shifts again, I can feel his thighs between my legs again. I hear the sound of a wrapper tearing. A condom. I should have told him I'd been checked already. I'm clean. I'm also on the pill. But I don't, the feel of his swollen hard tip of his cock pressing against my entrance taking my breath away. I reach down, wanting to touch him and he lets me, my fingers trailing along his sheathed length. So big, hot, and throbbing.

Our eyes meet. Did I tell him no complications? Silly me. There will always be complications between us, but it's too late for that now.

Benny rubs the head of his cock against my opening, easing it in slowly. It's as if he's making sure he's not going to hurt me. I moan, wriggling my hips, wanting him inside me, yearning for him to fuck me senseless.

Suddenly he slams into me and my scream is caught

in my throat as his need meets mine. His ache for my ache. His mouth finds mine and I hear him groan, primal and unchained. Benny pushes my thighs wider, my knees sliding wider apart as I do my best to take all of him. He's big, filling every part of me. He begins to thrust and I bring my arms around him, wanting to hold him but Benny takes my wrists and pins them on the bed. He raises his head from mine, his eyes holding me hostage as he thrusts again and again. He's back in control and I welcome it. I crave it.

"Is this what you want?" He murmurs in my ear as he seats himself deep inside me, grinding his hips.

"Yes," I gasp as I wrap my legs around his waist. Why did I wait so long for this moment? Why did I let so many years come between us when we're perfect together. I'm light to his dark and he completes me.

"Do you like it when I take you like this? Rough and hard?"

"Yes," I gasp again. "Please, Benny."

He slides out of me, leaving only the tip of his cock against my entrance. I whimper, feeling the emptiness at his retreat. But I also see the cocky smirk on his face and I know what's coming. He slams into me and I scream, my voice hoarse as he fucks me harder, his movements speeding up as if it were right on the heels of my oncoming orgasm.

When my release comes, I bring my head back but Benny brings his hand to my face, bringing my head forward so I'm looking straight at him.

"Look at me when you come, Sarah," he orders, his thumb caressing my cheek as he continues to thrust into me. And then it comes, rolling like a wave and taking me with it. I scream Benny's name, not caring who can hear us. I've never allowed myself to be this open, to be this vulnerable but with Benny, it's the only way to be. My body tenses as my world shatters all around me. I feel my orgasm take over, my arousal spiraling again as he pounds into me, my body squeezing, clenching around his glorious cock.

Benny growls in my ear, nips the skin of my neck as his body tightens. I feel his cock throbbing inside me, swelling and pulsing as he comes with a roar, his voice vibrating against my skin. My heart swells at the sound of his release and when he lets go of my wrists, I cling to him, the muscles of his back rippling beneath my fingers. When he collapses over me, the weight of him is a comfort. It feels like home.

He always was.

CHAPTER TWELVE

Benny

I CATCH MY BREATH AND GAZE AT SARAH'S FACE, HER skin glistening with perspiration. She looks so beautiful, so content... almost dazed as she catches her own breath. I can hear my heart beating inside my chest, like wild horses galloping across the plains. I remember watching them as a child new to the reservation, wild and free.

Outside, the wind picks up, rattling a neighbor's roof. Two cats shriek in the distance. A dog barks. I close my eyes and rest my forehead on Sarah's, inhaling the scent of her, a memory I want to protect forever, both of us as one.

I kiss her on the lips, sharing one breath as she sighs. My chest tightens, a question settles in the pit of my belly.

"Benny..." she breathes and I silence her with another kiss, deeper this time. I don't want to hear anymore, not when my heart is telling me something I've long denied to myself.

I've always loved Sarah Drexel.

I slide out of her, roll onto my back and get up from the bed. "I'll be right back," I say, needing whatever remnant of solitude I can find to get a handle on my feelings. I've only been denying them for so long and right now, they're requiring my full attention.

In the bathroom, I clean up, wrapping the condom in toilet paper and tossing it in the trash. Washing my hands, I stare at my reflection in the mirror, knowing I can't stand here forever. I need to get back to Sarah. I need to hold her in my arms.

I hear her cell phone ring as I step out of the bathroom. I pick it up from the floor next to her jeans and hand it to her before crawling back into bed and pulling her to me so we're spooning. She looks at the display but doesn't answer.

"Who's Enrico?"

"He's Melina's son," she says, silencing her phone and setting it on her bedside table. "He's been wanting to go out with me since he stopped by the clinic four weeks ago."

I nuzzle my chin in the soft curve of her shoulder. "Are you planning on seeing him?"

Sarah turns to look at me, a curious expression on her face. "Would you like me to?"

I bite her skin playfully and she giggles, goosebumps

dotting her skin. "Would you like me to mark you as mine?"

"But I'm already yours, Benny," she whispers, rolling onto her back. "I thought you knew that."

I kiss the spot that I bit seconds earlier. "Just checking."

"Can I make sure you're never going to forget?" Sarah sits up, biting her lower lip as she studies me in the semi-darkness. Outside the window, the full moon illuminates her skin, revealing the soft slope of her shoulder, the generous curves of her breasts, and the dark shadows of her nipples. Her rumpled hair reveals a halo of yellow as she moves slowly between my legs, her movements smooth like a cat.

"How do you plan on doing that?" Even as I ask her, my cock stirs as Sarah wraps her hand around the hardening shaft. She lowers her face before my cock, her hand tightening and loosening at the base as her other hand cups my balls.

"Like this," she murmurs, licking her lips slowly as my cock twitches in her hand.

"I'm not that easy, you know."

She grins. "I know that. You play hard to get very well."

"Not if you ask nicely," I say, folding my arms behind my head.

"Please."

"Please what?"

"May I please suck your cock?" She asks expectantly, frowning when I don't answer right away.

"You're forgetting something, Sarah." As my voice emerges as a growl, she stares at me for a few moments, almost surprised. Suddenly, it hits her and her eyes widen. I can almost see her blush as the next word emerges as a whisper.

"Sir."

My cock is now standing in full attention, rock hard and throbbing. I press her palm against the shaft. "Ask me again."

Her nostrils flare, her tongue gliding along her lips again. "May I please suck your cock, sir?"

This time, it's my heart that's hammering inside my chest, the sound of her voice saying such words making my stomach clench. "Yes, you may, Sarah," I murmur as she lowers her face and plants a kiss on the head of my dick, right on the drop of pre-cum glistening along the tip. Then she swirls her tongue around the head of my cock before sucking gently and I almost lose myself.

Watching her do everything I say almost becomes my undoing. I want to grab the back of her head and push her down my cock, forcing her to take me all in her mouth. After all, isn't this what she wants? But I don't. Those things take time and right now, I want to take it slow... or as slow as we're taking it right now which isn't exactly the truth. We're simply making up for lost time.

Sarah rests her hand on my hipbone, her palm warm on my skin, her mouth circling my cock even warmer.

She works her way down, moving slowly, inch after inch. I gather her hair in my hand so I can watch her, my breath caught in my throat. She feels so good I know I won't last long.

"Sarah..."

"I want to make you come, Benny," she whispers as she looks up at me. Then she runs her tongue along the underside of my cock from tip to base and back up again. I let go of her hair and lean back on the pillows, closing my eyes so I can feel everything. Her hands, her mouth, her tongue. Her submission.

I can feel my cock swell in her mouth, my release so close. I open my eyes and watch her go up and down my cock, as deep as she can and then pull away. It's a glorious sight and I know I'm not going to last any longer.

When I come, she takes all of me in her mouth and this time, I reach down to hold the back of her head. It's a light hold, just enough to let her know I want her to remain where she is and she doesn't fight it. I groan, my body shuddering as I let go, my body taut as a wire. I gasp, feeling her mouth still around my cock. I let go of her hair and collapse on the bed, needing to catch my breath. I don't have to look at her to know she's licking me all over, my shaft, my balls, the head of my cock. She's cleaning me.

Fuck. That's all I can think of as I Sarah plants a trail of kisses up my torso, her hair feeling like butterfly wings on my skin. As she runs her tongue around one sensitive nipple and the other, I chuckle, pulling her higher so her face is in line with mine. I wrap my arms around her, our bodies molding together as one. She's so beautiful, my nizhoni. My woman.

I pull her face toward me and she hesitates, her brow furrowing. "But Benny, I just.."

"I don't fucking care." I pull her face toward me and kiss her, our tongues tangling, tasting as my hand drifts down her back, my hand grabbing her ass and squeezing. She moans against my mouth, pressing her body to mine, grinding her hips before I lift my hand and deliver the first spank. She gasps, her eyes widening as she stares at me.

Then she laughs a throaty laugh and I bury my face in the curve of her neck, inhaling the scent of her, memorizing her and knowing there's no turning back now.

I'm so fucking done for.

WE FINALLY GET out of bed two hours later, famished. I put on my clothes so I can run to the truck and get the container of food that Nana had packed for me. Sarah is exhausted, her voice hoarse from her cries, but she insists on frying eggs while a plate of enchiladas warm in the oven. As I fight the urge to wrap my arms around her as she cooks, I can see the marks I left on her wrists and her neck. I've never been this rough with anyone and at the same time, I've never been with anyone who wanted it this rough either. Sarah craves it like air. She was soaking wet the moment I held her down, her body humming with anticipation as I took control of her.

"How do you like your eggs?" Sarah asks and I tell myself to set aside all thoughts of lovemaking. For now, food takes precedence over everything else.

Later, as Sarah watches me lazily from across the dining table, our plates empty, I realize I haven't torn my eyes away from her. I simply can't get enough of her. She's like a drug I've always wanted, a temptation I never succumbed to because I knew I'd be done for if I did.

Well, I'm done for. One taste of her lips and I was hers. And in that moment when I claimed her, we were one. One breath. One Heart. One soul.

"Something's bothering you," Sarah says, her fingers stroking my forearm snapping me back to the present.

"I was just thinking how perfect we fit together," I say as she traces one of the tattoos on my skin. *And how we shouldn't.*

"Sarah, I left marks on you," I murmur, pushing a lock of her hair behind her ear.

"Nothing a little concealer can't hide." She kisses the back of my hand, her lips moving up my wrist and forearm.

"I don't want people to think I'm hurting you."

"But where's the fun in that when it's what I want?" She asks, chuckling as I lift her chin.

"I'm serious, Sarah. Shiprock is a small town and the

people, they see marks like this all the time, maybe in other places, on a woman. And they think one thing."

Sarah frowns. "That's the last thing I want them to think about you, Benny. Ever. I know you'll never do that."

I kiss the back of her hand. "Next time I'll be more careful. I'll put marks where no one can see but us."

"I'd like that," she says as I kiss her mouth next, the feel of her lips on mine making my cock stir. We've already gone twice before this and I want to go again. I want to claim her and make her mine. But I also know there's a time for everything and right now, it's bed. I also need to hold her... just hold her as if making sure she's really here with me, that she's not leaving.

"Why don't we head to bed? You're tired."

"So are you, but first I have to clean up. I'd hate to wake up to a mess in the morning." Sarah gets up from her chair and starts gathering the dishes. She doesn't object when I help her and we get everything cleaned and put away in fifteen minutes. We've always been a good team and two years apart hasn't changed that. One scrapes the plates clean while the other rinses them, passing them back to the other so they can be arranged in the dishwasher. It's a simple routine but it's as if we know what the other is about to do, a synchronized partnership begun four years earlier and now maturing into something else.

The moment we crawl into bed, sleep takes over but not before Sarah nestles her body against mine and I wrap my arm around her. Her breath feels soft and warm on the skin of my arm. I kiss her shoulder, inhaling the scent of her hair and skin and wishing I could bottle it.

Tomorrow I'll need to make a decision. I can't keep living a double life, with one foot planted on the land of the Diné and the other on the land of the white man. I remember when Mother had to go through a five-day ceremony just so she could step back into her family homestead after Dad died. I don't remember the details—cornmeal, ash, chanting that lasted for hours, days—I'd been too terrified and too young to understand what was happening less than two weeks after Dad was killed, his sister being the one to handle all the funeral arrangements because Mother was too afraid to deal with his death. She feared his ghost would haunt her dreams and when they did, when her nightmares began shortly after, that's when she decided to go home to seek help. But the one thing I remember the most was the sight of my mother emerging from the ceremony so cleansed of the ghost of my dead father, she never uttered his name again. He was a ghost who wouldn't bother her anymore.

I wouldn't see a picture of Dad until I received a packet containing my trust fund information a few weeks before my eighteenth birthday. Even then, Mother refused to look at it. She didn't need to. The moment I looked at his picture, I realized she saw him every time she looked at me. Everyone did. No wonder my stepfather couldn't stand looking at me and did everything he could to make me regret being born. I reminded him of the man who took his woman away.

But that was then and this is now. Although I do as much as I can for my clan, I know I can do so much more, like living on the reservation, marrying a Diné woman and raising a family together. Noelle was always that woman whom I could live that future with.

Too bad my heart begs to differ, more so now as I watch Sarah stir in her sleep.

I pull her closer, feeling her hair brushing against my face. Will I be a ghost to my clan, too, when I tell them that I've never stopped loving a white woman from the moment I met her? Or should I simply end this now before I hurt Sarah like all the other men before me?

CHAPTER THIRTEEN

Sarah

Benny is gone when I wake up but he left me a note on his pillow. As I read it, I can smell his cologne on my pillows mingled with a scent that's all his own. The memory of the last few hours makes my stomach clench and I press my thighs together.

I miss you already.

I chuckle, my voice throaty from last night as I roll onto my back and stare at the ceiling. I touch my nipples under the sheet, the skin still sensitive from Benny's attention. Closing my eyes, I let my hand drift down my belly, remembering how his beard tickled me as he kissed me, especially down there from my belly to my thighs and between my legs. My fingers slide lower, grazing skin that hasn't forgotten Benny's touch. I sigh. If only he didn't have to go to work.

The buzzing of my phone on my bedside table snaps me out of my daydreams and lazily, I glance at my phone display wondering if it's Benny. The moment I see the three letters flashing on my screen, I grab the phone and hit answer. Some calls you just have to take no matter what.

"Hi, Dad. What's up?" I try to sound upbeat but there's no hiding the sound of my voice. It's hoarse and clearly coming from someone who just woke up at ten in the morning. In Dad's world, that's way too late to still be in bed.

"Can you take time off work to fly to New York and meet with your lawyers?"

I rub the sleep from my eyes, willing myself to be alert. "I was hoping we could work with my current schedule."

"Then that's what we'll have to do," he says. "I have a meeting with Lionel when I arrive in New York today and his people will try to work around your schedule. If not, you'll need to take time off. I don't think we can delay this, Sarah. Can you email me the dates you're off work today?"

"Give me a few minutes, Dad." I sit up and get out of bed. At my desk, I open my laptop and turn it on. It takes a few moments to get started, my muscles tensing at the memory of the last time I'd switched it on to look for pictures of me online. I've never hated the internet so much.

With Lionel Chambers handling my case, I know I'm lucky that this whole thing happened in New York. It'll make it easier for the lawyers to do what they need to do, not having to deal with different states and all that. But then, what do I know about legal matters when Dad takes care of everything?

"Lionel knows people who can track down where the listings with your picture and information are being posted," he says. "Something like forensics, but for the internet. He barely knows the details to break it down to me correctly but as long as he's got the people who can, that's fine with me."

"I'm really sorry about all this, Dad. I hope everything at the house is fine."

I hear him exhale. "No more apologies, Sarah. You've done enough of that since this whole thing blew up and it's high time you stop blaming yourself and trying to fix it on your own. Right now, we need to stop him from posting anymore and causing harm and that's going to mean hiring lawyers."

I want to ask him how much it'll cost but I don't. Maybe when I meet with the lawyers I will, but for now, I've got other things on my mind. "How's Mom?"

"She's doing well," he replies, chuckling. "She and Nana are having a blast entertaining the security guys. They're probably feeding them sopapillas as we speak."

I smile, the vision of Mom and Nana plying the tough security guys with food. I got to meet them yesterday morning, two former Navy Seals who now work for a private security firm that guards millionaires and billionaires. Not that Dad is one. He just manages their money.

"And Dax?"

"Dax is good," Dad replies. "He and Gabe are friends again. But then, when can those two hold a grudge for more than one night? They're connected at the hip."

I smile. "I think Gabe's his wing man... or whatever they call it when they play those online video games."

"Yeah, there's that. Gabe's his real life wing man, too, when you think about it." He pauses when someone asks him something and I realize he's already on a plane. I hear the sound of china tinkling, as if someone is taking an empty cup of coffee from Dad's table.

"Is Ryan still calling my old number?"

"Not just him, but a lot of sick bastards," Dad replies stiffly. "I don't listen to them but Fred from Trident does. He says I'm better off not hearing what goes through sick men's minds."

He's referring to Clyde Fredricks, an old friend who owns a security firm based in the East Coast. He hires mostly veterans and is even working in the field although it's light duty, guarding some rich socialite and her son around New York.

"They can keep calling all they want and say the things they want to do," Dad continues. "It's all recorded and traced. Every single one of them. So you need to always be vigilant and aware of your surroundings, Sarah, okay?"

My throat tightens. I may be on a high from spending the night with Benny but there's nothing like a reminder from Dad that there are so many crazies out there to bring me back down in an instant. But he's also right to do so. Ever since I took the job in Shiprock, I've let my guard down, confident that no one would find me here, definitely not Ryan who'll I'll probably spot a mile away. Like Benny says, he'll only stand out.

"I am," I lie.

"Your address over there isn't listed anywhere, right?" Dad asks.

"No, just at work since they're the ones who recommended this place." *I'm a ghost*, I want to tell him. *New cell phone number, new email. Zero presence on social media. No life.*

"What about your running? You still doing that alone?"

"It's just behind the medical center, Dad. A lot of people use it and when I take the ones around the area, I make sure it's during the day."

Dad exhales. "All it takes is just one person, Sarah. I suggest you stop that for awhile. Maybe run at the gym instead. Use the treadmill. Does your apartment complex have a gym?"

"No, but that's fine. I'll see about the gym." I want to tell Dad that I'm really okay running out here but I know it's not the answer he wants to hear.

"I just want you to be safe, Sarah," he says. "You know how I hate the very idea of you being alone out there. If this idiot found you in the last two jobs you got assigned to, what's to stop him from finding you out there?" He pauses. "And it's not just him I'm worried about. It's the crazies who find your pictures online."

I return to my bed and hug a pillow to my belly, that familiar feeling of helplessness settling in the pit of my stomach. "I'm so sorry you have to deal with this, Dad."

He exhales. "Oh, Sarah, don't ever think it's your fault because it's not. Any self-respecting man knows better than to do something as vile as this. And for what? All because you broke up with him?"

"But I can't hide forever, Dad," I say. "I can't let him do this to me forever."

"And that's why Lionel's firm is taking care of this even if it takes years," Dad says. "In fact, that's what his IP attorneys have told him already, that nothing like this has ever come up before. With the Internet being the wild wild west, they say it will take some time to stop completely. Years, maybe, so I want you to prepare for that."

"Okay."

"I want him to pay, Sarah," Dad continues, his tone harsh as he lowers his voice. "And I'll do anything—anything—to make sure he pays for this."

In the background, I hear a woman tell Dad to fasten his seatbelt because as soon as they receive clearance, they're landing at JFK airport.

"I've got to hang up now, Sarah," he says. "Don't forget to email me your schedule so I can get the flights chartered."

"Dad..."

"Yes, Sarah?"

"Thank you," I say softly. "Thank you for everything you do for me."

He doesn't answer right away and I can almost see him smile, or I'm hoping he's smiling. God knows how many times I've fucked up every time I try to do things my own way.

"You're welcome, Sarah Banana," he says and I know that smile I imagined was spot on. "You're one tough cookie. I know you are. That's why you tried to fix this yourself. But we'll put an end to this together, you and me. Okay?"

"Okay."

I hang up and stare at the wall beyond the bedside table. I suddenly feel light, as if a weight has been lifted off my shoulders. I close my eyes and sigh, grateful for everything that I've been blessed with even if most times, I have no clue. There'd been so many things I took for granted until the day came when the simplest thing, like walking out of my apartment without a care in the world, became an impossibility. And for what? Because a man couldn't take the sting of rejection.

And now, with him posting my home address and phone number, he's turned it into something bigger, like a pebble tossed into what was once a calm lake, its ripples growing ever wider. This time, it's not just my safety he's threatened, it's my family's, too. My mother's sense of safety once again shattered even if she hasn't said a word about it.

Déjà vu.

But no, this won't be a repeat of what happened to my mother in New York when one man's obsession turned deadly, driving her all the way to Taos. Too bad that's all I know about it for Mom and Dad refuse to talk about it and neither will Nana. It's a chapter best left in the past.

I return to my desk and pull up my schedule for the week. I've got four straight days of work ahead and three days off right after. I could wait until my days off but Dad's right about needing to get the ball rolling with the lawyers. I pull up my email client and type out an email to Melina requesting a few days off.

As I click Send, I let out a deep sigh. For the first time since this all began, I can finally see the light at the end of the tunnel. I can see an end to the fear I've been living with for the past year.

How can I forget the feelings of helplessness, fear, and paranoia that came over me the first time I realized what Ryan had done, that pictures he'd taken of me when we were figuring the whole BDSM thing out would be out there in the open for all to see? Did he really find rejection that difficult to accept, that he'd have to punish me the worst way he knew how? Breaking my trust in him and humiliating me?

I knew the moment the first phone calls started coming in—hearing raspy voices from strangers telling me all the things they wanted to do to me—that talking reason with Ryan was pointless. And just when I decided to call Dad and tell him what happened, it was too late. He found out through a colleague at the private club he went to a few times a week, a club with a rich history of the rich and famous being among their members. It meant if one knew, others did, too. When he told me, it put me on the defensive and our talks, no matter how rational and calm they'd start, turned into arguments... until yesterday.

Thanks to Benny talking me into giving it one more try with Dad, I've come to realize that no matter what happens, Dad—and my family—will always be there for me.

Maybe even Benny.

CHAPTER FOURTEEN

Benny

I HATE DOING WHAT I'M ABOUT TO DO BUT IT'S TIME. After six years of seeing each other on and off, surely I'd know if she's the one for me by now. But I'm also fooling myself to believe that's really why Noelle and I have been dating for so long, even after she must have known about the many women I'd been seeing back in Albuquerque or wherever I'd travel for work and we just happened to be "off" then.

It was never about love.

As misplaced as it was, it was about duty. It was about making up for the decision my mother didn't make when she ran off with my father a week before she was supposed to marry Ray. Just like Noelle, Ray had been her childhood friend and their families used to do everything together growing up. Sure, they loved each other but in the end, Mother ran off with my father, an older non-Navajo she met at a dance.

Arranged marriages may no longer exist among the Diné but certain informal arrangements still do, just like the one my mother and grandparents made with Noelle's family. If the kids liked each other, why not? If they shared the same interests—books, movies, a passion for all things Diné—why not?

I just never felt the same things I felt for Noelle the moment I set my eyes on Sarah—my heart thundering inside my chest just like wild horses made the ground beneath your feet tremble as they galloped across the plains, or the way my gut clenched at the sight of her and suddenly, I couldn't speak, the words caught in my throat, my mouth dry.

It was only when I told myself Sarah would always remain a friend that I was able to have my wits about me whenever she was around. As her friend, life was good. Not perfect, but good enough. I could talk to her, spend time with her, laugh with her until the time came when my body no longer reacted the way it did in the beginning. It certainly helped that I'd convinced myself that Sarah was the one woman I couldn't have.

Only I've just had her. All of her. And there's no way I'm letting her go now.

The students are running around on the playground when I park the truck in the lot in front of Noelle's school. I've been here before and know the principal and a few of the other teachers. I've been to her classroom more times than I could count, usually before school started to help her decorate and on the last day, to take things down. Once or twice a year, I showed up to talk to the students about what I do as an environmental protection specialist.

Noelle and I go back a long time. She was the first real friend I had after Dad died and I suddenly found myself in a new place, a new classroom, immersed in a new culture. I was bullied then—a lot. It seemed as if everyone knew what my mother had done, that she'd abandoned her Navajo culture when she fell in love with a white man and had me. If Ray wasn't beating me up at home for some little infarction that day, the kids finished the job.

But it wasn't all bad. Even though her older brother Isaac was wary of me and my city ways, I found a friend in Noelle. With our grandparents already close friends, we often met at the chapter house whenever there was something going on. Noelle is soft-spoken and beautiful, with long dark hair and dark eyes. She was my first kiss and my first time just as I was hers. As my mother loves to remind me, *you and Noelle go a long way, Bidzii. You make a perfect couple. You'll have beautiful Diné children.*

We'd probably have gotten married right after high school if I hadn't learned of the trust fund my father had set up for me when I was born, an account that automatically transferred to his sister Melody Turner after he was killed in a car accident. My mother didn't even know anything about it.

After my father's family lost their case to get full

custody of me after my father's death, Melody would end up depositing money she and my paternal grandparents would have sent me for Christmas and my birthday into that trust fund. I wouldn't learn about it until I turned eighteen and I found myself looking at documents showing a balance that was more than anything I'd ever seen, more than my teenage mind could comprehend. It also contained a few photos of my late father holding me in his arms as well as his wedding band which I wear on a chain around my neck, much to everyone's initial horror and then later, disappointment.

Although my mother would have preferred me to use the money for other things we needed more—a new truck or repairs for the homestead—she knew I'd be the first one in her family to finish college if we followed my father's wishes. Sure, as a Native American I could attend college for free, but what about the expenses related to school? Living expenses and all that? And so after the initial four years, I set my sights higher, telling my mother that my goal was to earn a Master's degree and then later, a Doctorate. So whenever I told her I couldn't possibly think of marrying Noelle because I needed to finish my education first, she didn't push it... until she met Sarah by accident.

It had happened on a trip to Chaco Canyon where I showed Sarah the stars and then on a whim, we took an out-of-the-way detour to Four Corners where one could stand on all four states—Utah, Colorado, New Mexico, and Arizona. On the way to Taos, we ran into my mother and Ray and to this day, I can never forget the look of shock and disappointment on my mother's face. That's when she realized the real reason why I'd kept making excuses for not coming home on the weekends... or proposing to Noelle who at that point had been my on-again-off-again girlfriend for two years.

Four years later and I still hadn't proposed. Noelle had to give me an ultimatum and even then, I ended up bailing.

So why did I tell my family I was getting back with her just weeks after I told Noelle I wasn't ready to get married? I should have known Mother would run with the news and tell everyone she knew. If I'm such a man of my word, why can't I follow through with this one?

Because you love someone else... even when you shouldn't.

Still, I need to close this door once and for all. I need to move on and let Noelle do the same.

I get out of the truck and walk toward the security gate. Noelle should be having lunch right about now, which means she has time to talk to me. But as I raise my hand to punch the code on the panel, I see her on the playground and I stop. Wearing a red dress and ballet flats, she's tending to a little girl who's fallen, dusting the girl's knees with her hands before standing up. As the girl takes her hand and follows her into the building, probably to the school nurse, my chest tightens.

Do I really want to tell her that we're truly over right now, right in the middle of her workday? What for? It's not like she doesn't already know where I stand when it comes to us. There is no us, not even if my mother insists there is still hope there.

My phone rings and as I pull my phone from my jeans pocket, I see Tony's name. As I head to my car, I click answer. "What's up?"

"Hey, it's short notice, but we've got a trip to DC in two days, my man!" He says, laughing. "You, me, Collin, and David," he continues, adding the names of the other other guys in the team that worked on the paper on uranium mining.

"What for? We already gave them everything they needed. I know I did."

"The representatives want to ask us a few questions," he says. "Maybe clarify a few things, I don't know, but hey, it's a trip to DC. I've always wanted to check out the Smithsonian."

I get behind the wheel but don't start the engine. I'm supposed to be visiting my mother and helping around the homestead. I'd also been looking forward to talking with my grandfather. Instead, I'll have to push that back to the following weekend. Again.

"Send me the details and I'll make the arrangements when I get back to the office," I say as I see Noelle standing behind the gate. How long has she been standing there? "Hey, man, gotta go."

"I thought it was you," Noelle says as I approach. She steps out of the gate and gives me a brief hug. "What are you doing here? Everything okay?"

"I've come to apologize for my mother," I say. "I understand you ran into each other and she told you I had something to tell you."

"You don't have to apologize for her, Bidzii. But she did say that you had something important to tell me," Noelle says, smiling. "She kinda hinted what it was about but since I haven't heard from you in awhile I figured maybe it's just wishful thinking on her end."

"I told them we'd get back together," I say, clearing my throat.

She frowns, her eyes narrowing as she studies my face. "Does she know about my ultimatum?"

Either you ask me to marry you or we break up for good, Benny, she'd said. *I want a family with you, little versions of you and me running around our home...*

I can still remember how the room felt like it were spinning, her words fading as if I'd suddenly gained wings and was flying far away.

That was two months ago and in a moment of weakness—or maybe regret because it meant I went back on a promise to myself to stay on the reservation—a few weeks later, I told my family something I didn't mean.

"No, she doesn't. That's between you and me," I reply. "But I'm here because I don't want to apologize or explain things over the phone. I want you to hear it from me."

Noelle doesn't speak for a few moments. "She's back, isn't she? That girl from Albuquerque, your friend from UNM?" When I don't answer, she continues. "Isaac saw you with her the other night in Taos. He and his friends went to see that new Navajo band playing at the Pit and he told me he saw you two dancing. He said you danced with her all night."

"I didn't see him." Not that I was paying attention to the crowd. I had eyes only for Sarah that night.

"Doesn't matter if you did or not. It is her, right?" Noelle's tone is accusing. "The same girl you brought up to the Four Corners that one day you two ran into your mom and your stepdad?"

I nod. "Yeah, same girl." Normally I'd have added that Sarah is just a friend but I can't do that now. She's more than a friend. And according to the way my gut tightens, it's been that way for a long time. I just couldn't admit it then.

"I figured as much. You really did like her. You tried not to show it, but I could tell. That's when you came back to me for real, after she left and I really thought that was it." For the first time, I see a pained expression cross Noelle's face. She takes a deep breath and exhales through her lips. "But it's been two months since we broke up, Bidzii, and it's not like I've just been sitting around waiting for you to come to your senses."

"I'm sorry, Haseya," I say, calling her by her Diné name which means She Rises. "I never meant to lead you on."

"We had a good run," Noelle says, her smile not matching the sad look in her eyes. "But we can't fool ourselves into believing it'll work when the last six years has shown us that it can't. I want to live here on the res, Bidzii, but all you want to do is leave it. It's always been that way ever since…"

"Ever since what?"

"Ever since you got that envelope in the mail," she says, her gaze moving down to my chest, at my late father's wedding band. "Ever since you put your late father's wedding band on a chain around your neck and hardly ever take it off." She pauses, taking a deep breath. "Oh, I've seen you put it away sometimes because you know it upsets me, but it doesn't change things. He's dead, Bidzii. I wish you'd understand that."

"It's the only thing I have that belonged to him." The words leave my mouth through clenched teeth.

"Yet it goes against everything we believe in," she says softly. "That's why his ghost never leaves you. That's why you always want to go out there, to prove yourself to the world that you're as good as he was."

"Because he was and like it or not, his blood runs through me," I say quietly. "Does that go against everything you believe in, too?"

"No, because you're still a Diné no matter what," Noelle says. "You know our ways, you've lived our ways. Yet the day you got his wedding band… the day you let it hang on that chain right above your heart, you invited his ghost in and you've been conflicted ever since. Even your mother and your stepfather say so."

Suddenly I'm back at Noelle's apartment, the world no longer spinning for something told me there was more she wanted to say. There was more to the ultimatum she'd just given me.

Before you give me your answer, there is one more thing, Bidzii—

I'm not taking it off, Haseya. I'm not getting rid of it.

Not even for me?

It's the only thing I have of my father. And whether you like it or not, I'm still his son, I'd said, fighting back the panic, the memory of the last time my stepfather tried to wrestle the chain from my neck when I came home with it the first time. That would be the last time Ray would lay his hand on me, the day I fought back and almost killed him.

You'll always be his son, Bidzii, but you don't have to wear his ring to know that, she'd said. Your heart already knows. Besides, he's dead.

I still can't, Haseya. I'm sorry.

The school bell rings and I'm suddenly back in the present, my hand wrapped around my father's wedding band, as if protecting it. At eighteen, my finger wasn't big enough to fit the ring but now, it fits perfectly. He was my height, maybe a bit taller, with jet black hair and a thick beard, his eyes a combination of blue and gray. He was young and ambitious and during the six years he was with my mother, he gave her the world. They traveled all over Europe and kissed in full view of the Eiffel Tower. He gave her flowers every week, sunflowers, being her favorite. He even serenaded her and she'd turn beet red and beg him to stop. But he'd keep going anyway. All this

I'd never have known if I hadn't received that envelope containing my trust fund information, his pictures and the ring. And thanks to my Aunt Melody telling me the stories my mother never did, he came alive in my mind.

Only to the Navajo, he was a ghost that no longer belonged in this world. And in many ways, I was one touched by one as well. Wasn't that why Mother and I went through days and days of ceremony to rid us of his ghost after he died, me especially?

It's something we never talk about but I'd been in the car with him when the drunk driver hit us and we careened off the embankment. They wouldn't find us for another six hours when someone finally noticed the tire tracks and spotted the car below. By then, Dad was dead and I was stuck in my car seat, unable to get out. I don't remember much, but to my mother, I'd been touched by the dead, even if it was my own father.

Noelle hurries back to the gate and punches the code to unlock it. It buzzes loudly.

"I thought maybe you'd changed your mind, that you'd finally understand..." As Noelle looks at me just before walking through the gate, her eyes are no longer pleading. I see sadness instead, even pity. "Goodbye, Bidzii."

"Goodbye, Haseya."

She knows where I stand... where I'll always stand, and not even her final ultimatum will change that. One foot in and one foot out. Always straddling two worlds when I could easily choose just one.

But I'm not going to make that choice—not today, not tomorrow—not if it means letting go of the only thing my father ever owned that's now mine. Too bad the mere act of wearing a dead man's ring goes against everything Noelle and my family believe in.

I get in my truck and pull out my phone. There's a message from Sarah but I set it aside to read later. I need to take care of a few things first.

Everyone needs to know this chapter in my life is over even if it means learning that Benny Turner is a man who goes back on his word.

CHAPTER FIFTEEN

Sarah

THE MOMENT MELINA APPROVES MY REQUEST FOR days off, I email my updated schedule to Dad. I'll still be working tonight but the next five days I'll be off so I can meet with the lawyers. It all depends on Dad, of course, but I find out three hours later when his email arrives.

Lionel is making this case a top priority for his firm. You should be receiving an email from them shortly informing you of what you'll need to take along with you to the meetings. It won't be a smooth ride, Sarah, but I can stay with you the entire time if you want.

I've also enclosed your flight schedule. The charter will be taking off from Santa Fe. Email me if you have any questions.

I text Benny and tell him about my travel plans, where I'm going and who I'm meeting with. I figure he'd at least want to learn that I'm moving forward. I'm fighting back. I wait for a few minutes for a reply but nothing comes. Tossing the phone on the bed, I tell myself he's working. He'll get back to me later. But the moment my phone vibrates, I grab it and check my messages.

I'll be out of range for a few days. Will reply as soon as I get a signal. If this is an emergency, call the office.

I tell myself not to worry, that Benny's being Benny. Back at UNM, being out of cell phone range usually meant he was visiting family on the reservation. It meant a weekend not seeing him. I survived then, didn't I, even though we were just friends then? He's living his life just as I'm living mine.

Still, a part of me worries. *Is he having regrets?*

True to Dad's word, the email from Chambers, Maynard & Lipman arrives an hour later detailing everything I need to bring with me. After a quick shower, I spend the next two hours gathering all the evidence I'd collected since I broke up with Ryan. Copies of text messages, emails, and even recordings of his voice messages, first when he was trying to reconcile and later, when he realized I wasn't coming back. The change in his voice and demeanor had been chilling then. From a man in love to a man scorned. By then, I'd filed a restraining order against him after I found him waiting for me by my car at work. Shortly after that, the pictures would surface online and the hospital would let me go because the photos and online postings violated the morality clause of my hiring agreement. I didn't even fight it. How could I? My colleagues could barely look me in the eye after that. To them, I'd become the sex-starved woman they saw in pictures online, tied up, gagged and according to the accompanying text that included my phone number, begging for more.

As much as I hate to play back the tapes, I also include the voicemail messages from strangers who'd found my "listing" online detailing all the things they wanted to do to me. I remember having to buy an old answering machine that still used audio tapes just so I could have some sort of record. And sure enough, I do, their voices sending chills up and down my spine as I fast forward the tape until the end. How many of these tapes did I end up filling up before I gave up and canceled the auto-forwarding of all calls and handed my cell phone to Dad?

With trembling fingers, I open a folder containing printouts of the posts with my naked pictures along with my "message" asking for anyone interested in a good time followed by my phone number. I remember when Ryan took the pictures and within seconds, I find myself back there, feeling helpless as he promised me the pictures were only for us. For him. He simply couldn't get enough of the sight of me so submissive, so helpless.

I break into a cold sweat, willing myself to return to the present. There's no way I can go back there alone. I take one last look and close the folder, stuffing it along with a disk drive and all the cassette tapes into my carry-on luggage.

Dad is right. This isn't going to be easy.

CHAPTER SIXTEEN

Benny

AFTER LETTING THE OFFICE KNOW THAT I'LL BE taking the rest of the day off to take care of personal stuff, I stop by my apartment to grab a change of clothes and four five-gallon water jugs before making the two-hour drive to the family homestead.

Even though the water lady comes by every two weeks to fill up every water container my mother can find in the house as well as the troughs for the sheep, with six people living on the property, there's never enough water to go around. While one person uses about 80 to 100 gallons per day living in places where water is just a twist of the tap away, on the reservation it's a different story. Everyone in the house has to make do with about seven to ten gallons per day and that includes water to cook, bathe, and drink.

I got used to it growing up but it can't be like this forever. If I hadn't bought the townhouse last year, I'd have been able to have a 1,200 gallon cistern installed that'll be powered by the solar panels.

On the way, I stop by the supermarket and pick up a few things that I know Mom can use—Bluebird flour and Crisco for the fry bread she makes every day and coffee for my grandfather. I pick up other things, too, since I'm already at the store. Toothpaste, soap, shampoo, deodorant, and for my grandmother, a bag of sunflower seeds.

I arrive at my childhood home two hours later to find four of my nephews and nieces watching TV in the living room while my mother is in the kitchen. They're my cousins' kids who live on the same homestead, their trailer visible in the distance. Ever since I installed two solar panels that power up the appliances and the big-screen TV, my nephews and nieces hang out at the house more, turning my mother into their unofficial babysitter. But she doesn't mind. She loves the company and whenever she's in town, she buys DVDs that entertain them for hours. I do, too. I even bought a video game console for my twin brothers even though they can't play those online multiplayer games that are getting popular. But they have enough games on CDs to last them a long time.

Petite with long dark hair that she arranges in the Navajo traditional hair bun and wearing a red shirt over a pair of jeans, my mother's face brightens when she sees me. "What are you doing here? I thought you were coming in this weekend," she says, enveloping me in a long hug.

"I have to travel to DC tomorrow with some guys in the office. Last minute trip."

"You and your travelin', Bidzee," she says, shaking her head. "I hope you meet some senators."

"I doubt it. Probably interns." I close my eyes, inhaling the aroma of something delicious wafting from the stove. "You're cooking ach'éé?"

Sizzling in a pan, she's frying short lengths of sheep intestines wrapped around stomach fat, a Navajo delicacy that isn't exactly the best for me but I love it. I wash my hands in the sink and grab a piece before Mother can shoo me away. I bite down on the crunchy layer, the juices hitting my taste buds like an explosion of flavors.

"Your brothers wanted me to make it for them so they'd have it after school," she replies, wagging the ladle at me. "I know it's your favorite, too, so don't eat it all."

As the kids come over to say hello, I see my sister through the curtains making her way toward the house from the sheep pen.

"What's Marge doing here?"

"She had to get some things she left behind for her apartment and ended up helping your grandfather with the sheep pen," Mother replies as she hands the kids mini-versions of fry bread to take with them to the living room where a SpongeBob DVD is playing on the screen. "She'll be staying the night."

"That's good. I wouldn't want her driving at night," I say. "Ray at work?"

Mother nods. "You know he is, Bidzii. I know you

two don't get along but I hope you're staying for dinner. It's quite late already as it is."

"I'll take the couch," I say as my sister enters the house through the back door.

"Benny!" She shrieks before running into my arms. Eight years younger, she's a carbon copy of my mother. Her long hair is tied in a pony tail and she's wearing an AC/DC t-shirt under her checkered shirt, jeans, and work boots.

"Do you even know what AC/DC is?" I ask, releasing her as I eye her shirt.

"Of course, I do. I stole all your rock CDs but you never noticed because you were too busy studying for your next big degree."

I roll my eyes. "Yeah, right. Guess who's studying for *her* big degree?"

Marjorie blushes. "It's only a Bachelors, Benny. Look at you! You've got a Doctorate! Which reminds me, I should be calling you doc, right?"

"No, you better not." I pinch her chin playfully. "But don't knock your Bachelors. It's still a degree, and a damn good one at that."

Thanks to my father's trust fund, I've been able to help Marjorie with her college education. Even though she doesn't have to pay college tuition as a Native American, I cover the rest of her bills like her apartment and utilities so she can focus on her studies. With Ray spending every extra dime he makes on booze, covering Marjorie's expenses is also my big fuck you to all the years Ray beat the crap out of me, showing him that despite being the so-called demon living under his roof, I can do something he can't do.

"Do you have stuff in the back of the truck?" Marjorie asks and I nod.

"Just water and some groceries."

"Let me help you bring them in." She follows me outside to my truck where I hand her the bags of groceries.

After a few more pieces of ach'éé until Mother shoos me out of the kitchen, Marjorie and I spend the next two hours repairing sheep fences, chopping firewood, checking the solar panels, and anything else that needs fixing while we're both here. Tahoma and Tsela arrive home and help out, too, and even the kids up until my cousin arrives in her old SUV to pick them up.

I save the task of helping Granddad tidy up the hogan for last, enjoying the time he and I get to talk in private while everyone else joins my mother inside the main house.

Growing up, Granddad was the one who taught me the ways of the Diné. He'd wake me up at four in the morning and together with Grandma, we'd chant a morning meditation song while facing the sunrise with an offering of yellow cornmeal. At sunset, he taught me to offer white cornmeal. Every day he'd tell me stories about the Holy People, about Mother Earth and Father Sky, and about the Coyote. Sometimes Grandma would do string games to go with the stories, too, something that Marjorie enjoyed learning to do on her own.

But these days, we talk of grown-up things, about the state of the land and the air, about the contamination of the rivers with radioactive waste, and that of the air and the land, too, with uranium waste from the closed uranium mines, and how uranium made the water I grew up drinking taste sweeter than water I'd drink outside of the reservation. Little things that now remind me just how different I am from people like Sarah with her old moneyed father and privileged mother, daughter of a well-known potter.

Twenty minutes later, the kitchen table fixed and the screws on the chairs tightened, Granddad and I head to the main house for dinner. The sight of my stepfather sitting at the table takes me by surprise but I don't show it. I knew this was coming.

"Hey, Benny," he says, rocking back on his chair as I walk in. "Nice of you to join us natives for dinner."

At the table, I do my best to enjoy the dinner of mutton stew and fry bread, aware that Ray is watching me closely. He looks amused to see me at the table, as if he can't believe his luck to find me under his roof again since I usually only come by on the weekends when he's passed out drunk somewhere else.

My siblings do their best to lighten the atmosphere. While Tahoma and Tsela talk about their latest video game, Marjorie tells us about taking her roommates to the Navajo Nation Fair where they got to watch the dancers and the crowning of that year's Miss Navajo Fair.

"Remember when you first danced at the fair, Benny?" Ray asks, the smirk still present on his face. "Didn't you partner with Noelle then? You with your red shirt and your brand new moccasins, looking all native. You even had a feathered cap." He chuckles, his hands above his head mimicking feathers. "That was cute."

"Stop it, Ray," Mother says.

"Stop what? I'm only trying to make conversation," Ray says. "Can't a man make conversation in his own home? It is my home, too, right? I mean, I paid the bills before Benny here started paying for things like that nice TV and pretty expensive solar panels."

"He's only helping out, Ray," Mother says.

"Noelle was Miss Navajo Nation Fair one year, wasn't she?" Ray asks, ignoring her. "I still remember you flying in from wherever you were studying for your college degree then. Florida or something. Man, she was so happy the girl was glowing. Completely in love with Benny here."

"She was Miss Photogenic," Marjorie says. "She should have won the crown, to be honest."

"Thing is," Ray continues, "Noelle's been waiting for our Benny here to make up his mind. But word on the street is... he dropped the ball."

"What Noelle and I talk about is no one's business but ours," I growl.

"Oh yeah? Her mother called her dad today at the

plant. She was so upset. Said you paid their girl a visit at the school and dumped her. Officially," Ray says, gloating as everyone around the table stares at me. "Isaac told them why. Wanna tell us why, Bidzii?"

He says my name mockingly, and for as long as I remember, he always believed I didn't deserve a Navajo name.

"Is he telling the truth?" Mother asks, her face pale. "Did you break up with Noelle when I thought you said..."

"I changed my mind."

"You changed your mind after you told us?" Tsela asks, his eyes wide. His twin brother looks at me in disgust.

"Man, that's cold," Tahoma says.

"Isaac was in Taos the other day," Ray says and everyone stops talking to listen to him. "Said he saw Benny here dancing with that white girl he brought up here years ago. That's true, right? Said you never even saw him." When I don't answer, he continues. "Guess she's the one who left that hickey on your neck, huh? Or what do you kids call that now... a love bite?"

"My personal life is no one's business," I say, getting up from the table, my appetite gone.

"It is when you tell us you're finally going to ask the poor girl to marry you and then you change your mind. Again," Ray says, getting up from his chair. "Only a coward changes his mind around here. Only a coward says one thing and does another."

"Ray..." Mother says but Ray ignores her.

"You know who does shit like that?" Ray points his fork to everyone at the table, as if he's giving a sermon. "The white man. They say one thing and then they turn around and do somethin' else. Usually backstabbin' you. Is that you, Benny? After all, you got half-white in you so why not–"

"Ray, stop," Granddad says and Ray glares at him, shaking his head.

"You defendin' him, too?" Ray says as everyone stops eating, their eyes avoiding his gaze. "Just because he bought the damn solar panels and a big screen TV and other shit? Or is it because he got himself those nice degrees on that wall that you all love to show off to everyone who comes in here?" He chuckles as Mother looks away. "Yeah, everyone lets Benny do whatever he likes. Romance a girl to get in her pants and then say he's not ready. Make her wait. Get another degree just because he can. Then get another. And another and another. I mean, with all that education, who has time to get married, right?"

I step away from the table toward the front door but Ray grabs my arm. Suddenly I'm a boy of seven beaten so severely that he left scars on my back and Granddad had to take me to the hogan he and my grandmother lived so I'd stay there instead. I grab the collar of Ray's shirt and raise my fist in a move so instinctive I realize too late that I'm no longer that kid whose simply fighting back.

"Shiyáázh," Mother pleads. *My son.*

"You wanna hit me? Go right ahead, Mr. Big Shot," Ray taunts. "You wanna show who's the king of the castle around here, Benny? Be my guest, the man whose word isn't worth crap."

I can feel everyone at the table watching me. Disappointment is written in their eyes. Tahoma and Tseya. Marjorie with her hand on her mouth, horrified at what she's seeing. Granddad and Grandma. My chest tightens and I let go of Ray and lower my fist, but it's too late. It's done. I'm the man whose word means nothing, the man who wears a dead man's ring on a chain around his neck.

"And so what you said the last time you were here... you didn't mean it? You lied to us?" My mother asks, disappointment stamped all over her features. Marjorie's expression goes from shock to disgust as the realization finally hits her. She'd gone into Elementary Education and specialized in Diné Studies because of Noelle.

"I meant it then."

"Yeah, right," Ray sneers. "And then he changed his mind."

"Be quiet." Granddad tells him sternly before facing me. "Is it true, Bidzii?"

"Yes, Shicheii," I reply, turning my attention to everyone at the table. "I spoke to Noelle this afternoon. She and I are officially over."

Everyone starts talking but I don't listen. All I see is my grandfather and the look of sadness in his eyes. I excuse myself and head toward the front door. I can pick up words here and there, the loudest of them Ray's.

He's a coward. Just like his father.

Ray, stop. Please.

That last one comes from my mother before I step outside, the night sky lit up with stars, more stars than I could ever count even if I had a lifetime ahead of me with nothing to do.

Coward.

The word stings deep, but that's how the truth works sometimes. It stings.

———

I COULD HAVE GOTTEN in the truck and drove home but it would have proven to everyone what a coward I really was if I did. But I'm better than that. I made a choice and I'm standing by it. I made a mistake and I admitted it.

So I walk around the house to my grandparents' hogan and sit in one of the plastic chairs outside their door. That's where Granddad finds me twenty minutes later.

"The First Man took great care to build the constellations because he wanted the work to be perfect as they lit up the night sky," Granddad says as he settles on the empty chair beside me. "Coyote watched him the whole time, waiting and waiting. He wanted to see the constellations, too. But he grew impatient and so when the First Man wasn't looking, he gathered the sheepskin where the stars were laid out and threw them up in the sky.

Because of his impatience, the constellations ended up in bunches that look so disorganized. But are they?"

When I don't answer, he continues. "Waiting for everything to be perfect is not the way you are meant to live this life. Too much thinking and not much doing is not good for you... like the coyote waiting for food only to go hungry. But you can still find beauty in imperfection, Benny. There is beauty in taking control of your life and going your own way. Even when the impatient Coyote threw all the stars up in the sky in no particular order, the constellations didn't turn out wrong."

As he talks, I spot *Náhookos Bi'ka*, the Big Dipper in the sky and I suddenly feel tired of having to read between the lines. "What are you trying to tell me, Shicheii?"

"We all have stories, Bidzii," he say as he pats my shoulder. "But sometimes stories are just that—stories—even the ones you tell yourself when you think you're alone."

CHAPTER SEVENTEEN

Sarah

THE NEXT MORNING, I DRIVE TO SANTA FE AS SOON as I get out of work. In the executive lounge at the Santa Fe airport, I shower and change into something more comfortable for the trip. I board the plane, falling asleep the moment we take off and wake up three hours later when the flight attendant announces we're about to land.

I used to think I'd always live in New York right after college but after the incident with the professor and then Ryan, there's nothing for me here anymore. My life is in New Mexico now, with Mom deciding to move there for good and now, Benny.

After his last message about not having cell phone reception, I haven't heard from him. He's probably with his family and if he is, I hope he's enjoying himself. I just wish he'd tell me more about them even if I'll never meet them again after that unfortunate run-in two years ago on our way from Four Corners. That's when I found out about Noelle because his stepfather certainly didn't hold back.

She's a friend, Benny had told them but it didn't look like they believed it. What made it worse was that he hadn't told them he was going to be in the area and I think that hurt his mother more.

But I can't keep thinking of Benny even if my mind chooses to default to the hours we spent together every time I close my eyes. I need to focus on why I'm making this trip, to begin the process of suing Ryan. For what, exactly, I have no idea but that's what the lawyers are for. All I have to do is answer their questions and give them all the evidence I have. Oh, and keep it all together while I'm at it.

Dad's waiting for me at the hangar and we have a late lunch at a one of his favorite restaurants in Chelsea. I'm always amazed at the New York version of my father where he's not as laid back as he appears whenever he's home in Taos. Today, he's still dressed in a tailored suit, although he'd long removed his tie, looking every inch like the Manhattan executive that he is, CEO of a growing investment firm that's slowly outgrowing its original offices in the Financial District.

There's no denying I'm proud of my dad, and a little intimidated, too. Without him working the long hours he does, we wouldn't have a beautiful home in Taos or the brownstone in Manhattan if Mom ever decides to set foot there again. I wouldn't have had a chartered plane fly me from New Mexico to New York in three hours or a chauffeured town car drive us everywhere we need to go.

"I was thinking we could head back to the house and I'll make dinner while you catch up on your sleep," he says. "You did just finish a shift, right?"

I nod, yawning. "Yes, and I had to drive to Santa Fe right after work."

"Then home it is after this and I'll take care of dinner when you wake up," he says. "That way you'll be prepared tomorrow. They need all the evidence to build an airtight case against this man, Sarah, and so we need to cover all our bases. It's not going to be a pleasant experience and I should have warned you about that."

"I figured as much, Dad," I say.

"Good. At least, we're on the same page," Dad says, smiling reassuringly. "Once they gather all the evidence, then we can build a case and bring it to the District Attorney."

I look at him, my face burning with shame. "Aren't you worried everyone will know about the pictures?" As if sleeping with my married professor wasn't bad enough, now this.

"Would you rather this man keep stalking you, posting your pictures online and having strangers tell you the things they want to do to you?"

"No, I want him stopped. Like yesterday."

"And that's why you're here." He squeezes my hand from across the table and lets go, leaning back as the waiter arrives with the appetizer. We're at the same restaurant he used to take me to once a week before Mom and I moved to Taos. It was our special time together, just him and me. I still remember how it always made me feel like a princess.

Only I don't feel like a princess anymore. I'm all grown up now. And I need to face my problems head on instead of running away from them all the time.

THE NEXT MORNING, Dad accompanies me to the offices of Chambers, Maynard & Lipman in Midtown Manhattan. I almost ask him to stay with me but I tell him to go back to his office anyway. I'm a big girl now. I can do this no matter how deeply it will take me back to the moment this thing all started all because of a bruised ego and naiveté.

Three hours later, I emerge from the conference room exhausted and fighting back tears. Although the whole process was professional and the lawyers did their best to ask as tactfully as they could, it was the answers that got to me, answers that told of a woman who fancied herself in love with a doctor because he was more than willing to fulfill secret desires someone else refused her.

Tie me up? Check. *Spank me till my ass was red and stinging?* Check. *Gag me and fuck me all while the cameras were rolling?* No, I never agreed to that last part. I didn't even know they were there until after the pictures started popping up online. After I found three of them on forums and have all my requests to have them taken down ignored, I haven't looked that hard.

But just because I told them where to find the pictures and videos—at least, the ones I'd found—didn't mean they stopped there. They'd been scouring the Internet the last few days looking for any footage that resembled me... and found more than a dozen of them. A few minutes here, a few minutes there. All in all, almost half an hour's worth of footage. Half an hour that could ruin my chances for getting a job at any hospital.

They must have seen the look of shame on my face the moment I realize just how much they had found online or the way my voice seems to stop cooperating with me and all I can do is clear my throat yet nothing comes out. Maybe it's the way I feel my body fold into itself afterward and I feel like I'm floating above everything else, as if I'm invisible. It's probably why the lawyers cut the interview short and suggest we meet again in the morning.

"That'll give us time to go over everything you've given us so far and our people can go through the time stamps on all the footage," the head lawyer whose name escapes me says as we make our way down the hall to the main lobby. I'm glad he doesn't say anything else to try and make me feel better. It's all business and that's how I like it.

We'll take care of everything, Miss Drexel. You just make sure to be safe and vigilant.

But when I see Dad emerge from one of the offices at

the end of the hallway, my throat tightens when I see Lionel Chambers step out of the office behind him. They're in the middle of a conversation but they stop when they see me, both men smiling.

Although his smile is fatherly—I've known him since I was child and he was one of my godfathers during my baptism—the feeling of shame that filled me just minutes earlier in the conference room returns.

Had he seen my pictures, too?

"There she is," Dad says as he approaches. I smile weakly, knowing that if I don't, I'll probably burst into tears. But I can't do that. No, I need to hold it together.

"Hi, Dad. Hi, Mr. Chambers." Those five words are all I can manage before Dad pulls me alongside him, squeezing my shoulder.

"You look exhausted."

"I am. And all I did was sit there."

He shakes his head. "You did more than just 'sit there', Sarah," he says. "You're building your case against this monster. One that will set an example to anyone else who thinks they can do what he's doing and not suffer the consequences."

"This case could take years but this brave young lady here is doing the right thing," Lionel says.

We say our goodbyes and Dad guides me down the hallway toward the lobby and into the elevator. It's as if he knows how hard the last few hours have been for me and he just wants to get me out of there.

The rest of the ride back to the brownstone where I

spent the first eight years of my life goes past me in a blur. I don't even know if Dad said something or not. I just know right now, I'm a shell and I want to be alone. I need to be alone and I'm glad that Dad senses it. He doesn't talk during the drive there, instead spending the time going through his calendar while Dave, his driver, navigates the busy streets of Manhattan.

When we arrive home, I go straight to my room and close the door. I collapse on my bed and curling up into a ball under the covers, I let the tears finally flow. I don't even know why I'm crying but I can't stop myself. I haven't felt this ashamed since the first time I found out what Ryan had done.

But I also can't cry forever. I can't let Ryan defeat me like this.

An hour later, freshened up and wearing flannels, I go downstairs and find Dad in the kitchen closing the oven door and setting the potholder on the counter. He's out of his three-piece suit and with his hair still damp from the shower, is wearing a heather gray t-shirt and a pair of black jogging pants. His laptop is open in front of him, a small camera clipped to the top.

"Thought Mom and I would make you your favorite. Macaroni and cheese," he says when I pull up a seat on the kitchen island across from him.

"Need any help?" I ask as he shakes his head.

"Thanks but I'm almost done. Just had to check." He turns his attention to the laptop sitting on the counter. "Your mom came up with recipe and directions."

On the screen, I see Mom sitting at the kitchen table back in Taos, Nana preparing something in front of the stove behind her. This is how they've managed to still be together during the weeks Dad has to work in New York. For Mom who was never into electronics, it's one thing she's learned to use in the years since they've been living apart part time. It's not something that happens every night since Dad often hangs out at the Metropolitan a few nights a week talking business but it eases the separation between them.

"Hi, *mija*," Mom says, waving at me. Behind her, Nana approaches the camera and waves as well. "I hope your meeting today went well."

"It did," I reply, my feelings of helplessness and shame now gone. I want my mother to see me confident. I don't want her to worry about me. "Where's Dax?"

"He's playing his video games in the entertainment room with Gabe and Claudia." She cocks her head toward the direction of Dax's bedroom, a knowing look on her face. Claudia Romero is Gabe's cousin and she also happens to be my brother's first love although Dax refuses to admit it. His face turns all red every time any of us mention her name but he clearly likes her. He just likes his video games more some days. Guess with Claudia visiting again, they must be seeing each other again. "So your dad tells me you go back to the office in two days?"

I nod. "Hopefully they get everything then and I don't have to come back again after that."

"But even if you had to come back, like for the court for example, if it ever makes it to that point, I'll be with you throughout the whole thing," Dad says.

"Me, too," Mom says and Dad and I look at the laptop screen, surprised.

"Mom, you don't have to," I protest as Mom leans into the camera. She's never returned to New York since she left it eighteen years ago.

"For you, I will, *mija*," she says, her smile fading from her face. "No one messes with my little girl."

I look at Dad but he doesn't speak. His Adam's apple bobs as he swallows and he nods.

"Very well, then," he says before turning away to get something from the fridge but I have a feeling Dad doesn't want me to see his expression.

Dax, Gabe, and Claudia enter the kitchen and join in the conversation. There's no more talk about the case. This time, it's about Dax and what his plans are for college which haven't changed. While Gabe is eager to start working on his general education classes at the community college, Dax hasn't decided what he wants to do. He wants to take a "gap year," he tells us and adds that if British kids could do so, why couldn't he?

"Because you're not British?" Gabe says, rolling his eyes. Behind him, Claudia has found some chicharrones that Nana made to snack on.

"Maybe it's time you go home, man," Dax says as Nana reminds him that Gabe and Claudia are staying for dinner and the conversation shifts to what Gabe and

Claudia's plans are for the future. The next half hour until the macaroni and cheese is ready to be taken out of the oven is spent laughing and catching up on what's been going on the past week since Dad flew back to New York. It's always been this way since Dax was born, two houses for one family, one of them constantly filled with so many people going in and out and the other, quiet and almost solitary. Just Dad on the screen.

As I watch my parents laugh at something Claudia says between bites of more chicharrones, I realize that once upon a time, I'd have given everything to return to New York—and I did. But not anymore. I want the former now, a home filled who people who love each other, no matter how noisy or rowdy they may be at times, a home where the only language that's spoken is love no matter how difficult it can sometimes be.

And selfishly, I want Benny in it, too.

CHAPTER EIGHTEEN

Benny

I MAY BE ADVENTUROUS—AFTER ALL, I'VE SKY-DIVED, bungee-jumped, and driven on a closed course—but driving from DC to New York City to surprise Sarah? Nope, I'm not that adventurous or crazy for that matter, not when I know nothing about Manhattan and I'd probably end up making a wrong turn somewhere and face the wrong way in rush-hour traffic.

And so I get on a shuttle bus filled mostly with Korean tourists returning from an overnight trip to check out the national monuments. It meant having to turn down joining the guys on a tour of the Smithsonian on what would be our last day in DC before we flew home but the moment someone at the hotel mentioned that there was this private company that ran a shuttle between New York and DC and they just happened to have a bus leaving in two hours, I was all for it, last-minute be damned. Besides, with the work we'd set out to do all completed, I couldn't wait to see Sarah, if she was still in New York. After all, I've already seen the Smithsonian.

And so shuttle bus it is.

I find a window seat toward the back of the bus, pull down the trucker cap I'd bought just for the occasion over my eyes and do my best to pretend I'm asleep.

After a brief goodbye to everyone still in the living room after my talk with Granddad, I'd left my mother's house that night, making the two hour drive home just after midnight. Although I felt like a weight had been lifted off my shoulders, I also felt like crap. I'd failed everyone and not even my grandfather's talk could make me feel like I did the right thing.

After working so hard to be what everyone wanted me to be—the son who'd end up walking the path of the Diné—I'd let everyone down. I'd let my emotions get the best of me, taking over duty and everything else.

But I also couldn't keep beating myself up over my decision. I'd made up my mind and the only thing I could do from here on was move on. And that's what I did—got on a plane to DC with the rest of the guys and did the work I was supposed to do. Talked with one or two representatives, answer all their questions to the best of my ability and simply focus on work.

But work isn't saving me from thoughts of Sarah. Even though I made the decision I made with Noelle for me, there's no denying that Sarah is part of that reason, too. I want her more than anyone I've ever wanted before.

And I'm done telling myself I can't have her. It worked during those two years at UNM but not anymore. Not now. If anything, this last-minute trip will tell me where I stand in her life, that is, if I manage to actually surprise her. If she's still in New York.

Three and a half hours later, the bus stops in front of a Midtown Manhattan hotel and we all get out. Slinging my backpack over one shoulder, I sprint down five blocks to get to the offices of Chambers, Maynard & Lipman. Thank God I memorized the name when Sarah first told me or it wouldn't be a surprise.

With my shirt sleeves rolled up to my elbows revealing my tattooed forearms and sweating from my sprint, I step inside the dedicated elevator for the legal firm. Last minute is something I never do but there's a first time for everything even if I don't look too hot at the moment. I need a damn shower after that sprint but I don't care. If Sarah is still in here, then it'll all be worth it.

I exit the elevator and find myself in an ornate lobby, leather couches and wood coffee tables, a large arrangement of flowers covering my view of the receptionist's desk. A different world, a different tax bracket.

I walk up toward the wide circular desk where a lone woman sits facing a computer, the security guard standing next to table straightening up.

"What are you doing here?"

I look to my right to see Daniel Drexel seated at the

end of one of the leather couches, a newspaper opened in front of him. He folds it closed and after glancing at his watch, gets up and heads toward me.

"Sarah told me she'd be here." I shake Daniel's outstretched hand, wishing I'd taken the time to stop by the hotel and take a shower.

"What are you doing in New York? This isn't exactly close by, is it?" His grip is firm, not as firm as it was in New Mexico but his eyes narrow as he studies my face.

"No, it's not. But I was in DC and I thought I'd surprise Sarah."

Daniel doesn't say anything. He only looks at me with narrowed eyes although his mouth isn't set in a grim line. But he's not smiling either. "You like my daughter," he says after a few moments. "And not as a friend anymore, I gather."

It's not a question. It's a fact.

"I do, yes. But I'm here because I wanted to give her some moral support." Only that's not quite true. I want to do more than just give Sarah moral support but there are certain things you can't say out loud in certain company, like Sarah's father.

"You do know why she's here, yes? You do know what happened with her... ex-boyfriend?" Daniel asks and I nod.

"Yes I do, sir, and that's why I'm here. I'm also not like the other guy."

Daniel smiles faintly. "I never said you were. Anyway, I just got in myself about fifteen minutes ago.

Thought I'd take her to dinner. Maybe a stroll along South Street Seaport," he says. "Ever been there?"

I shake my head. "No, I'm not that familiar with the city." In fact, I'm not familiar with New York at all. I'd spent most of the ride from DC memorizing the area of Chambers, Maynard & Lipman just so I'd find it on my first try. Avenues run south to north and streets east to west in Manhattan apparently. All I needed was knowing the five square blocks that separated the hotel where the bus dropped off their passengers from the legal offices so I wouldn't look like an idiot in the big city.

"How long are you going to be in town?" Daniel asks as I follow him to the couch.

"I fly back to Santa Fe tomorrow."

"Definitely a very short trip then," Daniel says as I set my backpack down on the floor between my legs. "You're lucky she had to come in for an extra day. She would have been done yesterday but according to the attorneys, there might be a civil case as well."

"A civil case? What about a criminal case? What this guy is doing, posting her naked pictures online–"

"There is currently no state law against this... this type of thing, Benny. Revenge porn is the word I hear being bandied about," Daniel replies, his jaw clenching. "But that doesn't mean there are ready-made answers to deal with it. No, it will take time and she just might have to accept that until this is over, no hospital might want to hire her."

"I'm sorry to hear that."

Daniel shrugs. "That's why we're all here, isn't it? We're here to put a stop to it."

"But the cost–"

"Cost is nothing if it means Sarah will be safe," he says. "Anyway, you should accompany Sarah and me for dinner–"

Daniel doesn't finish what he says for the door at the far end of the lobby opens and Sarah steps out. Carrying a folder in one hand, she's wearing a fitted black top and dark slacks, a scarf around her neck and her hair tied in a loose pony tail. She looks so beautiful I forget to breathe.

Sarah stops in her tracks, her eyes widening when she sees me. My name escapes her lips followed by what I can only call a shriek and she runs right into my arms.

I get up from the couch just in time to catch her, all formality with her father forgotten. Her arms around my neck, her body pressed against mine, she's here with me and for a moment I forget where I am. I inhale her scent, her beauty. I take her in.

It's been too long.

"Oh my God, Benny! What are you doing here? I thought you were in... wait, seriously, what are you doing here? Shouldn't you be in..." Her words tumble from her lips so fast but before I can answer, Daniel clears his throat and Sarah extricates herself from my arms. She turns to her father, her cheeks reddening. "Hi, Dad."

"I've asked Benny to join us for dinner, honey," he says. "Is that okay with you?"

"Okay?! Of course it is," she says, pausing to look

between her father and me and back to her father again. "Have you been waiting long?"

He shakes his head. "Twenty minutes, tops. How'd everything go?"

Sarah's expression turns serious. "Better than yesterday. We were able to cover most everything and I'm pretty much done. It's up to them now."

"That's good to hear," Daniel says as Sarah wraps her arm around my waist, leaning her head on my arm. "Give me a few minutes. I need to speak with Lionel."

As Daniel is buzzed into the back office, I turn to Sarah and kiss her forehead. "You look beautiful."

"Thank you. And you're not bad yourself, Mister Turner." Her smile is radiant. "So, seriously, what are you doing here?"

"Surprising you," I reply as Sarah pokes me in the rib and I step back, grabbing her finger before she can poke me again. "Today's our day off and we're supposed to fly back tomorrow but instead of hanging out with the guys at the Smithsonian, I found a shuttle bus that goes directly to Midtown and here I am. Sweaty, but I'm here."

Sarah stands on her tiptoes, offering me her lips, soft and warm against my own. "I'll make you sweat even more later," she breathes just as the door opens and Daniel walks out. We separate, like two kids caught doing something we shouldn't be doing.

"You kids ready for dinner?" Daniel asks, his eyes telling me he knows what's up.

I take Sarah's hand, squeezing it. "Yes, Sir, we are."

"Good," Daniel says as he gestures toward the door. "After you two."

He takes us to the Paris Café which Sarah tells me is one of New York's oldest pubs. With its hand carved bar and rich history, its early patrons included Teddy Roosevelt and Buffalo Bill Cody back when it was part of the Meyer's Hotel, one of the poshest hotels in the area.

From our table, I can see the Brooklyn Bridge behind Sarah and she's honestly the only view that interests me as I steal glances at her while having a conversation with her father. Her smile alone is worth the cramped three-hour bus ride from DC.

After discussing the history of the pub, Sarah asks me what I was doing in DC and I tell them about the research results we presented to a few bored legislators and the desired outcome that I'm unfortunately not too optimistic about. Daniel is attentive, his brow furrowing as he listens, and I'm glad he doesn't interrupt me like many other men before him who usually can't stop keeping their opinions about Native Americans to themselves. Instead, he's curious, intent in learning what he can.

"Is that where you want to live one day? Back on the reservation?" he asks, stabbing a piece of steak with his fork. "You still have family there, right?"

"Yes, I do."

"Live on the reservation?" Sarah asks, frowning.

"I mean I still have family there," I say. "But living there, I'm not sure. I'm too settled in the city, I think."

"But you grew up on the reservation?" Daniel asks.

"I did, yes, after my father died when I was six and my mother returned to live with her family."

"I'm sorry to hear about your father," Daniel says. "That must have been difficult as a child."

"It was then," I reply, taking a sip of water. But I survived, I add silently as Sarah asks me if I've been to New York before. It's a change of topic that I welcome and for the rest of the dinner, that's what we talk about, New York and its history.

After dinner, Sarah suggests I show her the night life around the city while Daniel tells us that he's meeting Lionel at the Metropolitan Club for drinks. When he offers to have his driver take us around, Sarah declines, saying that she's doing the tour like a proper former New Yorker, on foot or via subway or yellow cab.

Outside, after we watch her father's town car drive away, I turn to Sarah, not quite sure what to make of her plans for the rest of the evening. "Are you really showing me the nightlife?"

She laughs, wrapping her arms around my waist as we make our way down the block. "Are you crazy? The only stop from here is your hotel room where I intend to show you what New York has to offer. Me."

"I love it when great minds think alike," I say, grinning as Sarah releases my waist to hail a cab.

From the moment we get in the cab, Sarah and I are

inseparable. She's by my side the entire time I check in, in the elevator and down the hallway to my room. Finally, when we're inside my room, the door locked behind us, she's in my arms, all of her. Mouths meet, tongues tangle, our hands explore as our bodies press together. She tastes of strawberries. Her hair smells of lavender. Her tongue is pure heaven and whatever self-control I'd promised myself a few days earlier is gone, completely gone. The first whiff of her perfume, the first taste of her lips and I'm lost. My cock strains against my jeans. How can I go on if this is the way she makes me feel? Out of control.

Sarah unbuttons my shirt, her movements hurried, desperate. I pull the elastic band of her hair and feel it tumble down her shoulders. I pull off her shirt and toss it on the floor. My mouth finds a spot between her neck and shoulder and she groans.

"Benny, you have no idea how much I've wanted this, dreamed it," she breathes. "It's been too long."

I suck on the sensitive skin behind her ear, her body shivering. "It's only been four days but tell me all about it. Your dream."

Sarah's hands continue down my torso, finding the button of my jeans, her fingers pulling down the zipper. "Every night I dream of this." She tugs my jeans down my hips, taking my underwear with it. I groan when her hand wraps along the underside of my cock, gliding softly over the sensitive head.

"And what do you do... in your dream?"

My cock bounces against her palm as she gets down on her knees in front of me, its tip glistening with my need for her. "This," she breathes as I lean against the wall, the feel of her warm breath along the head of my cock making me weak in the knees. "I dream of hearing you tell me what you want me to do. Claim me. Dominate me."

I groan as she wraps her hand around the shaft and strokes once, her eyes never leaving my face. Sarah licks across the head and I close my eyes at the sensations that hit me all at once.

"Will you show me, Benny?" She licks across the head of my cock and I suck in my breath at the sensations that hit me all at once. "Will you show me how it feels?"

I thread my finger through her hair, pulling her head away from my cock. As Sarah looks up at me, my stomach clenches at the look of submission on her face.

Control, I tell myself as I pull her head away from my cock, not ready to give in to her just yet. I need to take control.

CHAPTER NINETEEN

Sarah

"HANDS BEHIND YOUR BACK," BENNY ORDERS AND I do as he says. I want so badly to taste his need, pre-cum glistening at the engorged tip. I inhale just as he thrusts my face forward, his cock filling my mouth as I take him down into the back of my throat as far as I can.

Benny gasps, our eyes meeting, my gaze never leaving his face as he pulls my head away. He thrusts again and I do my best not to gag, my desire building higher and higher, spiraling as he controls my movements, his hands on the sides of my head, keeping me in place.

Making me submit.

Making me his.

But there's more than just submission on my part. I've never been this willing to trust anyone so explicitly in my life. No one has ever made me want to let go of my inhibitions like this but Benny.

He thrusts again, groaning as I take him all the way, my gaze never leaving his face.

"Sarah..."

Benny pulls away and pulls me to my feet. He kisses my mouth hard and deep, our tongues tangling, his hands unzipping my slacks and pulling them down my hips. It's only been four days since we were last together but it feels like four weeks. I'm hungry for everything he can give me, desperate to feel his desire to have me any way he wants.

He pulls me toward the console table right beyond the hallway and stands behind me, his arms around my waist. I see our reflection in the mirror. Benny's eyes are dark and intense.

"Look at us, Sarah," he orders, his mouth against my ear. "What do you see?"

My hair falls loose over my shoulders and my lace bar. His voice has me breathing hard, my heart racing. I

"Look at us, Sarah." he murmurs again, his beard scratching my neck. "Tell me what you see."

I frown, my mind struggling to shift gears. As his erection presses against my back, I know that raw physical need is a lot easier to process. It's why I preferred it for so long. No time to think and ruminate about life. Just... the moment. But this time, it's different. It's not just something physical, it's more than that. It's as if Benny is seeing right through me.

"Us," I whisper. "I see us, Benny."

His arms tighten. "It's always been us, Sarah. Did

you know that? We just never wanted to admit it, accept it. Instead, we danced around it, running away from it." He turns to look in the mirror. "Promise me no more dancing around the truth, Sarah."

"I promise." Tears prick at my eyes at the way his gaze strips everything from me, as if reminding me it's okay to shed all the armor I've worn all day as I found myself reliving my humiliation, my shame. So many pictures. So many video clips. How can I tell Benny about them without changing the way he feels about me, sees me?

"I love you, Sarah," he murmurs as I stare at him, wondering if I'd just imagined him saying those three words. "I've always loved you."

As I fight back my tears, I force myself to smile, make light of what he just said for surely he didn't mean it. How can he? "Benny, don't. It's ruining the mood."

He presses his mouth softly on my neck, his warm breath giving me goosebumps. "There is no mood here, Sarah, just the truth. I want you to know how I feel for you before we keep going any further. I want you to know I'll never hurt you."

I close my eyes as Benny presses his body against mine, his cock hard and hot against the small of my back. I rest my hand over his hand and move it lower, to the waistband of my lace panties.

"Then make love to me. No, fuck me, Benny. No need to be gentle. Be rough," I whisper as he slides my panties down. "I'm also on the pill so there's no need to–"

I don't get to finish the sentence. Benny bends me forward over the console table, positions his cock against my entrance and thrusts. There's no gentleness this time, not when I'm already so wet for him. I gasp as he buries his cock inside me, his fingers gripping my hair and pulling my head back.

"Look at us, Sarah," he orders and I open my eyes to the sight of us, unfiltered, raw, primal. He thrusts again and I groan, not caring who hears us. "This is us."

I moan, the combination of his words and the sensations that hit me so intense that my knees tremble. Benny brings my arms behind me, pinning me in place. It feels so raw, the look on his face as he takes me. Skin on skin. So primal, so deep.

I want to close my eyes but I can't. Benny growls, low and menacing, his gaze stripping me to the core.

Possessing me completely.

I see spots in front of my eyes, my body humming with an energy I've never felt before, building and rising like the tide threatening to take me away.

"You're mine, Sarah. All mine."

"Yes, Benny," I gasp, panting as he thrusts again and again. Below me, the console table rattles against the wall. I don't even care if there's anyone staying in the room next door. I don't care about anything but this moment. Benny with me, his grip tight around my wrists, making love to me. Marking me. Owning me. All of me.

"Come for me, Sarah," he groans as I come, my orgasm crashing into me like waves slamming against the shore. Again and again. Washing over me as if wiping the slate clean of everything else that came before this moment until there's nothing.

Just us.

It's always been us.

As he grabs my hair and pulls my head back, his mouth on my neck, being taken by him like this is exhilarating and almost wrong. But I love it. I love every minute and every second of it. It's my surrender, so complete and so visceral I feel like he's looking right through me as he claims me.

But there's also no denying why I feel the way I do. I'm in love with Benny Turner.

I always was.

When his release comes, the sound of his name filling the room is all I hear. That and the groan that comes from deep inside of him as I feel him thicken inside me, pulsing. And then he comes, releasing my arms and grabbing my hips, keeping me in place as a second orgasm barrels through me, built from his. My body shudders, trembles, my knees threatening to give way.

Still inside me, Benny slumps over me, his breath hot against my ear. I feel his teeth on my skin and I close my eyes. He's marking me.

"You're mine, Sarah." His arms circle my waist, both our bodies breathing in unison as I take in the scent of him, the feel of him, the essence of that part of him that's just for me.

"I've always been yours, Benny."

WE ORDER ROOM SERVICE AFTERWARD, too hungry and too tired to venture outside. There's no need anyway, not when it starts to rain, making the choice to stay under the covers the most ideal way to spend the rest of the evening. We don't speak of the transformation that just happened between us, an unmistakable shift in our relationship that's taken everything to a place we've never been before.

And for the first time since I've known Benny, I see his scars when he gets up from the bed to get something to wear from his backpack. They're old scars, criss-crossing his otherwise smooth back and just below his shoulder blades, I see circular marks, too, smooth circles that shouldn't be there. I don't need to ask him what they are. I've seen similar marks on a young patient at the hospital. Cigarette burns.

My throat tightens. The childhood he never talks about.

As Benny zips up his jeans, his brow furrows. "What's wrong?"

"Nothing," I lie as he pulls a shirt over his shoulders and walks back toward the bed. "Just ogling you, that's all."

"You're a terrible liar, you know." He playfully

pinches my chin. "If you're wondering, it was a long time ago. Another lifetime."

"I'm sorry."

"What for?" He asks. "Not everything's your fault, Sarah. Some things... well, they just happen and we move on."

"How can you?"

Benny shrugs. "I wouldn't be here if I didn't."

"But– "

"And that's all we're ever going to say about that, Sarah," he says as a knock on the door further ends the conversation. "That should be Room Service."

We set the dishes on the table by the window. Outside, the lights from the neighboring buildings appear only as muted colors as raindrops create streaks across the glass. I can hear the muffled sounds of the traffic below as the rain hits the window with every gust of wind.

My heart is beating so fast and I know there's no more denying what's happening as Benny takes my hand to his lips. I catch my breath, accepting the inevitable.

I'm in love with Benny Turner.

"When do you fly back?" I ask when he sets my hand back down on the table and proceeds to spoon vegetables on my plate followed by slices of steak.

"Tomorrow morning. But I want to drop you off at your father's place before I go to the airport."

I stab a piece of broccoli with my fork. "There's no need, Benny. I can find my way home."

He reaches across the table, lifting my chin with his finger. "I will drop you off in the morning."

I smile, my broccoli forgotten. The way his voice dips makes my stomach clench. I want to hear it again and again and again. "Okay."

Benny grins. "That's my girl."

We spend the next ten minutes eating, no words until we get food into our bellies. When I've eaten my fill, I set my fork on the plate.

"Benny, when my case goes public," I ask, "or if the pictures make it to Shiprock, how's this going to affect you? Your work? Your family?"

Benny doesn't answer right away. He leans his elbows on the table and studies my face. "I'll worry about my reputation and my family, Sarah. You worry about taking this bastard to court. You worry about winning, no matter what it takes or how long it takes. No matter what happens to me, you make him pay for what he's doing to you and your family."

"It could take years."

"I'm not going away, Sarah," he says. "I'll be right here. Team Sarah. No matter how long it takes."

"Promise?"

"I promise." He points his fork toward my plate. "Now eat up. The night's not over yet. You're going to need the energy to last until morning with me."

JUST LIKE HE PROMISED, Benny takes me home in the morning. Even though I'd texted Dad last night to tell him I was staying with Benny, he doesn't look pleased when he opens the door. But I'm also twenty-six, I almost want to tell Dad. I'm old enough to spend the night with a man.

But then, I've also got naked pictures and videos floating all over the Internet so I get Dad's annoyance.

"Good morning, Sarah," Dad says stiffly as Benny nods at him. "Benny."

"Mr. Drexel."

"Would you like a ride to the airport?" Dad asks. "My driver should be in shortly."

"No, thanks. I'm good," Benny replies before turning to face me. "Call me when you get back."

"I will."

"Goodbye, Benny," Dad says. "Have a good flight."

"Thanks, Mr. Drexel," Benny says. "Goodbye, Sarah."

After Benny leaves to catch his flight home, Dad turns to look at me, an eyebrow raised. Suddenly I wonder if I'm being foolish to jump into another relationship when I'm still reeling from the consequences of a previous one.

Am I making a mistake with Benny?

"I hope you know what you're doing, Sarah," Dad says as the service door in the kitchen buzzes and Dave walks in and wishes us a good morning.

I nod. "I do now."

CHAPTER TWENTY

Benny

MOTHER IS STANDING BY HER FRONT DOOR WHEN I arrive at the house. She must have spotted my truck on the road and decided to wait for me, her arms crossed in front of her.

She doesn't smile as I step out of the truck and for a moment I wonder if I'm still welcome in my old home. I don't think it'll come to that but if I'm not, I'll accept it. In going back on my word, I've brought shame to the family and the clan.

"Shi'ma," I say as I approach the house. Inside, I can hear my nephews and nieces laughing at something playing on the TV screen.

"What are you doing here, Benny?" Mother asks, frowning.

"I wanted to apologize to you for what happened when I was last here. The dinner," I say.

"Noelle came by two days after you were here, you

know," she says. "She said she found some things you left at her place and she was just dropping them off."

"She didn't have to make the long drive," I say, frowning. "I could have picked them up myself."

"She was visiting her family and so she figured she might as well stop by here, too." When I don't say anything, Mother continues. "You broke her heart, Benny. She waited a long time and she said she only had one condition if you two were going to be together for good. But you said no."

My father's wedding band. "I did."

"It's only a ring, Benny. His wedding band. Would it kill you to not wear it... and close to your heart for that matter?" Mother asks, sighing. "You know how our people view things like that."

Yes, I know how our people view death. We avoid it. We abandon a home if someone dies in it, never to enter it again. As poor as we were growing up, Mother never bought anything from a thrift store, afraid that its owners may have died. It's why she gave away all of Dad's belongings, thinking it was connected to her dreams of him—his ghost visiting her—along with my insistence at six-years-old that Dad was simply sleeping, that he'd wake up and come back to get me. I'd been trapped in that car with him for hours, begging him to wake up. I didn't know any better then.

"It belonged to my father, Shi'ma," I say. "You gave everything of his away. Or whatever Aunt Melody wasn't able to save." Like the pictures and Dad's wedding band.

"They were mine to give, not hers to take with her. She already had control of the trust fund as it was. Why should she get his things, too?" Mother pauses and sighs heavily. "But that's neither here nor there. I just don't understand why she had to include that wedding band in her letter to you about the trust fund. You changed after that. You started thinking differently."

"It's not because of the ring that I changed or think the way I do," I say slowly. "It's who I am. Don't blame it on anything or anyone else. It's me."

Mother takes a deep breath and goes back in the house but I don't follow her inside. Somehow, the place stopped being my home the moment I brought shame to its doors that night. It stopped being my home when she stood in front of the front door.

Mother emerges with a sports bag and hands it to me. "Here. Your stepfather didn't want it in the house but I hid it. Figured you'd come by."

"Thanks." I take it from her and watch her fold her arms in front of her again. "I wanted to take back the water containers so I can fill them up when I come back."

"Don't bother, Benny. We can get the water ourselves. It's about time Tahoma and Tsela start doing things around here anyway," she says coldly. "Besides, your stepfather doesn't want you in his house."

My throat tightens. *His house.* In our culture, it's *her* homestead, just as it was passed on from her mother. It's why I didn't want to jump into marriage with Noelle. It would mean leaving Mom and my half-siblings without any additional support. With Ray spending all his money on booze off the rez, they need me. Or maybe that's just what I tell myself. Maybe it's my way of making up for what I always knew would happen, me turning my back on my culture. My duty.

"What about you, Shi'ma? Do you think the same way as Ray?"

Mother's expression hardens. "You get rid of that ring and you can come back, Benny. Until then, stay away." Her gaze goes to my chest where my father's wedding band hangs on its chain. "I just want peace in my house for once. I'm tired of having to choose every single time."

Her words sting and for a few moments, I can't speak. But even if I can, what is there to say when your own mother turns you away? And I get it. Ray hates me and my guts. And now he's got another reason to hate me. I went back on my word. I brought shame to the family and the clan.

I want to talk to my grandfather or at least, say goodbye but I don't want to hear Mother tell me to leave again. The first time was bad enough. "Alright then. Tell everyone I said hello."

I turn away and head back toward my truck. I open the passenger door and toss my workout bag in the back seat.

"I hope she's worth it, Benny. You threw away everything that you are for her. I hope she knows that,"

Mother says as I walk around the front of the truck and open the driver side door.

"I didn't throw anything away, Shi'ma. I'm still the same son that you know," I say, the words hoarse. "I'm still Benny. Bidzii."

Tears glisten from my mother's eyes but her chin is held high. She shakes her head. "Just go before your brothers come home. You'll only make them upset."

I gaze at the homestead in my rearview mirror as I drive away until I can't see it anymore, the dust cloud forming behind the truck obscuring the view. But then, it could also be the tears in my eyes that almost fall down my face.

Only they don't, for to cry would mean Mother is right, that I'm making a huge mistake... that Sarah is a mistake.

But she's not.

Letting her go the first time was.

———

THE NEXT DAY, I hitch a ride with Tony to Santa Fe and meet Sarah at the airport. As she walks through the double doors toward me, her smile is so radiant I forget to breathe. And when she runs into my arms, I forget all my troubles.

"You have no idea how happy I am to see you," she breathes into my neck as she wraps her arms around me, not letting go.

"I'm happier to see you." As I hold her in my arms, I inhale her scent and everything that she represents to me from this moment on. Home.

There's no way I'm letting go now.

On the drive back to Shiprock, Sarah tells me that she's completed everything on her end as far as the situation with Ryan is concerned. The lawyers can't prevent any more pictures to pop up online but if they do, they've got steps in place to have them removed. She also tells me that a civil rights organization has stepped in as well although she doesn't know the details of what they can do. Everything basically will take time and she just needs to hang in there.

For the next two weeks, Sarah quietly settles into a routine. After she finishes her shift, I meet her for a run at the back of the hospital. She was right about the trail along the irrigation canal being popular with runners especially with a Suicide Prevention Marathon happening in a month. After the hourlong run, we have a quick breakfast at a local restaurant before we head to her apartment so I take a shower and get ready for work and she goes to sleep.

Some days we run along the trails around Shiprock and Farmington, including one that gives us a wonderful view of Tsé Bit'ai'í. She's still not keen on going out to dinner, afraid that someone might recognize her and I understand. In the meantime, I do my best to remain vigilant, keeping an eye on anyone who could be hanging around at her apartment or at the medical center during our runs.

And when we're not running or talking or cooking together, we're in bed, exploring and experimenting, learning new things about each other, seeing what works and what doesn't.

It's all I can do to keep my mind from thinking about my family and how things went down between my mother and me. Even Marjorie has stopped talking to me and it hurts. How could I have fallen so far, and all for a woman I thought I could never have... a woman I've fallen madly in love with?

Two weeks later, we drive to Taos to visit her family. This time, I don't get the second degree treatment from Daniel who also happens to be home, and for the first time, they invite me over for dinner.

While Nana and Pearl prepare the food and Sarah helps out with the salad, Daniel gives me a tour of the house. There are four bedrooms, a study, and a recreation room where one of the security guys uses as his bedroom while the other stays in the casita in the back. It's what Daniel calls the unattached home at the back of the house that's separated by an herb garden. And then there's a workshop attached to the garage where Pearl does her pottery. It's where we find Dax sitting on the floor, sanding a wooden box.

"What are you doing here?" Daniel asks. "I thought you were with Gabe."

"He's doing research on the computer. Says the

internet is faster here than at their house so I figured I'd come out here and make this while he does his homework." Dax holds up a wooden box with a lid that he lifts up to show off to us. "I made it two days ago at school. I'm gonna give it to Mom."

"You like woodworking?" I ask as Dax nods and hands me the box.

"I still have to stain it to bring out the grain," Dax says as I lift the lid and close it again. "And then it will be ready."

"How long did this take you?" I ask as I hand the box to Daniel.

Dax shrugs. "A few days. I'm still learning but Mr. Smith says I'm actually really good at it. He's my woodworking instructor at school."

"Do you like it?" Daniel asks.

"I do. It's... well, don't tell this to Gabe, but it's meditative."

"You familiar with joints?" I ask. "Mortise and tenon, that kind of thing?"

Dax nods, looking offended. "Of course, man. That's, like, basic stuff."

"Ever heard of Takeshi Woodworks? He's right here in town," I say. "He does Japanese joinery. Or at least that's what it's called. My roommate and I bought a table from him. No nails or glue. He just cuts the wood a certain way and joins the pieces together. Sturdy as any table held together with nails or glue."

"I've heard of him. Japanese guy. He's got a workshop close to the plaza," Daniel says, handing the box back to Dax. "Mom will love that."

"Yes, he does. You should check out his work," I say. "Long waiting list though. He might even consider taking on an apprentice."

Daniel looks at Dax who doesn't seem to have heard me, his attention on the box as he eyes it closely, as if making sure the surface is even. "Something to consider even though I'd rather he attend college."

Dax doesn't say anything. It's as if his attention is focused only on the box he holds in his hands.

"Trade school?" I volunteer, a suggestion that earns me a disapproving look from Daniel. But as his gaze returns to his son, he exhales and shrugs.

"We'll cross the bridge when we get there. Until then, he has to graduate high school first," Daniel says as Dax picks up a sheet of sandpaper and files one of the edges of the box. He's so focused on what he's doing that it's as if we're not in the workshop with him anymore.

"There you guys are," says Pearl from the door and I catch Daniel's face light up the moment he looks at her. "Dinner's ready."

Dinner with the Drexels is a noisy affair. Separated by a colorful array of New Mexican dishes that line the center of the table, I get to know Gabriel or Gabe, Dax's best friend who emerges from his bedroom telling everyone about the classes he'd like to take for his freshman year in college. Already he's planning on getting straight A's so he'll get accepted to med school.

Sarah sits to my left while Nana, sitting at my right, keeps adding food to my plate. She even feels my bicep when I'm not looking and I catch her giving Sarah an approving look.

When it has nothing to do with the food which is absolutely delicious, talk around the table revolves around Dax and Gabe's latest adventures, Sarah's work in Shiprock and whether she plans on extending, my job and my upcoming trip to Arizona for a conference before it shifts to Pearl's pottery and the next workshop she's holding at a local art studio. I also learn that Daniel has just finished moving his office to a new building. It's bigger and has a view of Manhattan and the East River. This weekend trip is his first in four weeks which Pearl says is too long for him to be away.

Daniel takes Pearl's hand and bring it to his lips. "It's the last time, *mi amor*."

"You promise?"

He nods. "I promise."

I turn away just before they catch me watching and smile at Sarah who saw the whole thing. But I can't help it. The way Daniel looks at his wife brings back vague memories of my father and the way he'd look at my mother. But that was a lifetime ago and she's moved on.

She's right. He's dead.

But I'll still wear his ring on a chain around my neck.

"Is this the way it is at your house?" Sarah asks. "With your parents? Is it this crazy, too?"

I want to tell her the truth, that it's not like this at all, but that's only because I'm there. I have a feeling the mood is probably more lively when I'm not, but I also don't want to dwell on the past.

This is my future now, should I choose it, with the Drexels and their wild and crazy household where Dax and Gabe rave about the latest video game they're playing, Nana can't stop feeling up my arm muscles, and Daniel still gazes at his wife like she's the only woman in the world.

———

AFTER DINNER, Sarah and I spend the night at my townhouse. With Mariano out of town, it means we have the place all to ourselves. While I go through my mail, Sarah stands in front of the entertainment cabinet trying to pick a movie for us to watch.

"These are all guy flicks," she says, pulling out a *Reservoir Dogs* DVD from the shelf.

"I doubt you'd find chick flicks here, Sarah," I say, chuckling as I return my mail back into the basket.

"Two choices so far," she announces, holding up two DVDs. "*Die Hard* or *Tombstone*."

I arch an eyebrow. "I've seen them both. Which one do you want to watch?"

"I've seen them both, too. But I'll pick *Tombstone*, hands down," she replies, biting her lower lip. "Besides, I want to be someone's huckleberry tonight."

"Doc Holiday's?"

Sarah stares at me, looking shocked. "Doc Turner's, of course!" Then she narrows her eyes. "In fact, I intend to distract you the whole time."

I chuckle. "You think you can actually distract me from watching *Tombstone*? Be careful. You just might lose."

"I bet you won't last a quarter of the way through."

I pull her toward me. "What do I get if I do?"

"Me."

"Hmm." I think for a few moments. "I think that's a good enough deal."

"Hey!" Sarah playfully swipes my arm, looking offended. "You'll pay for that."

"I can't wait."

I almost don't make it, but by the skin of my teeth I do. By the halfway mark of the movie, most of Sarah's clothes are on the floor and she's straddling me, doing her best to distract me as the action on the screen gets more exciting with every passing minute. She's managed to remove my shirt and unzip my jeans, the feeling of her lace thong grinding against my erection driving me crazy. Her breasts rubbing against my chest was bad enough.

It's taken all my willpower to last this long but I'm ready to let go. Watching Sarah go from being determined to getting frustrated when things don't go her way (even though they are but I'm not ready to let her win) is well worth the price of admission and now it's time I collect my prize.

"No more teasing," I murmur in her ear before

nibbling her neck and she gasps, her fingers digging into my shoulders as I move down her neck to her breasts, taking one nipple into my mouth and then the other. "Hold on to me," I murmur as she clasps her hands behind my neck and I lift my hips, pushing my jeans and boxer briefs down my hips, my cock finally freed from its confines and pressing against her thong. I push aside the fabric, my fingers brushing along her clit before I slip them inside, deep. Sarah gasps and I chuckle.

"Someone's wet. Very wet."

She moans when I press my fingers on her clit again, sliding them along her folds before slipping them inside again. "You were too busy reciting every bit of dialogue to notice, Doc Holiday."

"That's Doc Turner to you, young lady." I pull her to me with my other hand, capturing her mouth as I continue stroking her. She gyrates her hips as I move my fingers faster, loving the sound of her moans against my mouth and my tongue. She trembles, her fingers behind my shoulder, her nails digging into my skin.

"Benny," she gasps. "I want you."

"Show me how bad you want me, Sarah," I murmur as I withdraw my fingers from her clit.

She pulls away, licking her lips, breathing hard. Then she positions her hips over the head of my cock, her hand stroking the shaft, the head, before guiding it inside her.

"Fuck," I breathe, the feel of her pussy sucking me in, robbing me of breath. Sarah begins to move her hips, first in circles, her eyes heavy with desire, her gaze never leaving my face. Then up and down, slowly, taking her time.

She moans when I cup her breast in my hand. I take one nipple in my mouth, her body trembling as she continues to move, up and down, then in circles, gyrating her hips. As she moves faster, I can barely think. With my other hand, I grip her hips, guiding her as I thrust upward, pleasure mounting, building.

The sound of our breathing and our bodies meeting fills the room, the movie long forgotten though I can still hear it in the background. But I'm not listening. No, all I see is Sarah, her face, her breasts, her flat belly slick with perspiration as she continues to ride me. I'm so close and so is she, her pussy squeezing, tightening, throbbing.

I bring my hand up to her face, tracing her lower lip with my thumb. For a brief moment, it feels as if time stands still. I stroke her cheek, holding her gaze.

"I love you, Sarah."

She strokes my bearded jaw. "I love you, Benny."

I pull her to me and kiss her hard, our moans mingling as her body trembles with each hard thrust of my hips before surrendering to her orgasm and sweeping me along with it like the tide claiming what always belonged to her.

My heart. My soul. My life.

CHAPTER TWENTY-ONE

Sarah

"You're Sarah, right? From 4D?" A tall woman wearing pink glasses, her brown hair in curlers, asks me when I step out of the elevator. She's standing in front of the wall of mailboxes in the lobby holding three envelopes.

"Excuse me?"

"I'm Sandra from 3B," she says, shaking my hand.

"Nice to meet you, Sandra. Yes, I'm Sarah."

"You're the nurse, right?" She asks and I nod. "Someone came by to deliver flowers yesterday but you weren't home so no one could buzz him in."

I smile. Benny must have wanted to cheer me up. "He can always leave them in the lobby."

"It depends if the manager happens to be onsite, dear, but if I see them again, I'll tell them that," Sandra says as she clips three pieces of mail next to her mailbox.

"Thanks. I appreciate it."

It's been four days since Benny and I returned from Taos and he's been in Arizona for a conference ever since. He must have figured flowers would cheer me up after listening to me over the phone yesterday whine and complain about missing him and the routine we'd established the past few weeks. I can't believe how quickly I got used to it. The run behind the medical center right after work, breakfast of breakfast burritos with green chile at a nearby restaurant and then off to my apartment where he'd shower and change into his work clothes and I'd crawl under the covers, content.

Only I'm not content, not for the past four days since he left for his conference. His text messages and phone calls barely scratch the surface of how I feel for him, the ache deep in my chest that I've never felt for anyone before.

It scares me.

And so with every inch of exposed skin covered in sunscreen, I'm going for a run. It's better than lying in bed with my arm constantly checking the empty spot next to me as if Benny would somehow materialize out of thin air and fill it. As long as there aren't any delays on their drive back from the conference, at least, he'll be back by tomorrow morning.

I drive a few miles out of the city to an area where Benny and I ran a few times. It's on an Indian Service Route and it's a pretty straightforward trail that others use, too. Today, there are two other cars parked at the trailhead.

I set my watch, estimating my run will probably take me an hour which will give me enough time to return home, shower and get ready for work tonight. It's just what I need to clear my mind of many things. It also makes me happy especially when I hit the trails for it brings Benny back somehow. After all, he'd been the one to introduce me to them in Albuquerque. Before that, I'd only run on treadmills or the school track, too afraid to venture beyond the walls for fear that someone would recognize me. Back then, my affair with the professor had just happened and Dad was forced to get me out of New York. I lost friends and although Dad's colleagues were probably more understanding—I bet they started double-checking their own affairs after that—it still put Dad in an awkward position with clients probably wondering if it was his daughter that everyone at the club was talking about.

It wasn't as if I could continue attending college in Manhattan anyway, and so I had to find some other place to finish my degree. At UNM, Benny with all his swagger and reputation as a man-whore was the last person I could have ended up with, especially since we weren't sleeping together, but somehow it worked out. He liked hanging out with me just as much as I loved being with him.

We ran the trails together, we talked about life when we weren't working on papers and reports, and he taught me the two-step. One weekend, he showed me the stars as we shared a sleeping bag on the flatbed of his truck and he told me the story of how they came to be in his world, about Coyote who couldn't wait for the Holy People to arrange them in the sky and so when they weren't looking, he flung the buckskin across the sky and the stars that had been arranged on it so carefully scattered about, ending up wherever they did. When the Holy People asked Coyote why he did what he did, he told them he didn't like being left out. He named all the stars, too, and when one fell from the sky, he picked it up and named it So'Tsoh or Coyote Star and hung it on the horizon. Benny told me it's the equivalent to the Morning Star and to this day, I think of him whenever I see it.

Benny restored my trust in men. Sure, I'd end up breaking that trust when I showed up at his apartment drunk and wanting to try out certain things with him but that's the past now. What matters is that we're together again and this time, it's for real.

An hour later, I make my way back to my SUV. The other two cars that were there earlier are gone but there's another one parked right next to mine. I pull out my fob from my fanny pack and unlock the doors, opening the rear passenger door to grab a bottle of water.

"Sarah?"

I almost fall backward at the sound of his voice. I stare at him, unable to believe my eyes. He's wearing a white t-shirt and jeans, his blond hair hidden under a baseball cap. Aviator sunglasses hide his eyes.

I can't even hold the bottle of water. It falls to the

ground, its contents spilling, soaking through my running shoes. "Ryan, what... what are you doing here?"

"I wanted to talk to you," he says as I look around. There are no cars for miles. "I heard you're building a case against me."

I walk backward, keeping the SUV to my left as Ryan approaches. I reach for my phone from my fanny pack but don't pull it out. My hands are trembling. "You shouldn't be here. I filed a restraining order against you."

Ryan chuckles. "Oh, come on, Sarah. I just want to talk. Can't we talk? We used to talk a lot. You used to tell me everything. Every. Thing. Remember?"

"We broke up, Ryan. And after what you've done with those pictures, there's nothing we need to talk about," I say, doing my best to sound like I'm not scared because I am. "That's what lawyers are for."

"Ah, that's right. Your lawyers." Ryan chuckles dryly. "That's the problem, Sarah. Lawyers make things complicated. Did you know they've been at the hospital asking questions? Not only that, but their team of computer experts claim that they were able to trace from which computer the pictures were uploaded from and that they came from me?"

"Because the pictures did come from you," I say. "In fact, you posted the latest one with my home address. My home address! Why would you do that? It's been over a year since we broke up, Ryan. Let it go."

"Why won't you believe me when I say that my

laptop got hacked?" he asks angrily. "I don't know why you have to be a bitch about this."

"Tell that to your lawyers, Ryan." I reach for the door handle but he grabs my hand, knocking my keys to the ground. As I try to grab them, he reaches for me with his other hand and I take a step back. And another and another. My heel hits the curb and I fall to the ground.

Suddenly he springs forward, his fist slamming against my cheek and I see stars. My back hits the ground, the contents of my fanny pack spilling to the ground. My lip gloss, extra scrunchies, my phone.

He lunges again and I push him away, my nails digging into his face, his neck, his arms and he yells, his next punch landing on my shoulder and I roll away from him, fighting back the nausea that hits me. I scramble to my feet, gravel cutting into the skin of my knees and hands. I get up, fall down, and get up again, his fingers catching my hair, pulling my ponytail loose as I propel myself forward.

Suddenly I'm free and I keep running along the trail, barely able to see but I don't care. I need to get away. Ryan was never into running so he can't possibly keep up with me. I hear a car door slam and I speed up, panic rising. What if he runs over me with his car?

"Go ahead and run, you bitch," he yells as I step off the trail, stopping behind a boulder to catch my breath. My lungs are burning, the spot under my left eye stinging. "You think you can get me fired from the hospital?

Think again. I'm going to fight it all. I'll destroy you, Sarah."

I don't wait to hear anymore. I keep moving even when I hear the sound of something hard hitting glass. It shatters. But I don't stop to look back. I keep going. I keep running.

CHAPTER TWENTY-TWO

Benny

THE GUYS AND I LEAVE THE CONFERENCE RIGHT after lunch, foregoing any plans to meet colleagues for dinner for another day. We're homesick and I miss Sarah. We check out of our hotels, get in my truck and I hightail it back to Shiprock, even ignoring Tony's request to stop at another roadside stand selling jerky for the third time. I drop each one of them off at their homes and after a quick stop at the City Market for a bouquet of sunflowers, I head straight to Sarah's apartment, hoping to catch her before she heads to work. She's not expecting me back until tomorrow morning.

As I make my way to the lobby of her apartment building, a lanky woman wearing pink glasses opens the door before I can input the code on the console.

"Are those flowers for 4D?" She asks, poking her head out the door. "She said to leave them in the lobby."

"Who?"

"Sarah. The nurse. The flowers are for her, right?" The woman asks. "I told her about the other guy trying to deliver flowers yesterday but he didn't have the code for the building or her apartment number."

"What delivery?"

The woman looks at me, confused. "You're from the florist, right? One of the other guys said he was delivering flowers yesterday but she wasn't home." She pauses, her eyes narrowing as she looks at the sunflowers. "Come to think of it, he wasn't carrying flowers. Maybe they were in his car."

My throat tightens. "What did he look like?"

"Blond, tall, blue eyes. About thirty. Not your typical delivery guy, I guess, but good-looking. Always thought they'd come in a lot younger," she replies.

"Where did she go? Sarah?"

"She went out. Looked like she was going for a run," the woman answers. "But she drove."

I don't wait. I turn around and sprint back to my truck, tossing the flowers on the passenger seat. I don't know where Sarah went but blond, blue-eyed guys are not a common sight around Shiprock. And any guy who's supposed to be delivering flowers brings the damn flowers with them.

I could be wrong but I also have a bad feeling I can't shake the moment she mentioned the guy with blond hair and blue eyes. Ryan. Has to be. I should have known better than to leave Sarah alone. *How'd he find her? Where is she now? Where the hell did she go for a run?*

I dial her number. After five rings, the call goes to voicemail. I hang up and drive to the medical center first, scouring the parking lot for her SUV but I don't find it. She usually parks in the row closest to the jogging path and as I drive past it, her SUV isn't anywhere.

I drive to the college, wondering if she's running on the track there since I'm not running with her. She would have known better than to run the other trail outside of the city alone. But as I drive through the parking lot, I know I'm not going to find her here. My hand trembles as I dial her number again.

Sarah, pick up.

The call goes straight to voicemail. *Is the battery dead? Did she switch off her phone?*

I drive to the trail I've taken her twice in the past few weeks. It's off a service road that's popular with hard-core runners. Sarah should know better than to come out here alone but she's also stubborn. As I approach the trailhead, my heart sinks when I spot her SUV... or what's left of her SUV.

The windshield is shattered, the back windows completely gone as are the side windows, all of them bashed in. Dents and cracks mar the body, faint black specks sticking to the paint. A crowbar. As I walk around the battered SUV, my boot steps on something metallic and my stomach rolls. Her phone, its display shattered, desert sand stuck in the cracks. A few feet away, I see a tube of lip gloss.

"Sarah!" I look inside the car, fearing the worst, but it's empty. Shards of glass glisten from the seats.

Did Ryan follow her here and take her? Where do I even start?

"Sarah!"

I walk away from the SUV, scouring the ground for fresh footprints and stop when I see a pink scrunchie just along the beginning of the trail. I pick it up, looking around, searching. I call out her name again and again, louder each time, hoping she'd say something if she were still hiding. I fight back the tears, the sour taste in my mouth, the feeling that I failed her.

I keep walking along the trail, searching the landscape. It'll start to get dark soon and I need to find her. I check my phone for a signal but there's not a single bar. I call out her name again.

Then I hear it and my heart stops. I catch my breath. Gravel crunches beneath my feet as I run toward the sound. It's as if I can almost hear every piece of it under my boots. I listen, straining to hear what I thought I heard. Or did I simply imagine it?

I call out her name again. I wait.

"Benny?"

She emerges from behind a boulder and I catch my breath. She looks so small in the distance, her hair loose, her shoulders and arms red from being out in the sun. I don't need to know that she's afraid. I heard it in her voice when she called my name. I can feel it in my heart, twisting my emotions, wringing me dry.

I run toward her, navigating through the shrubs of snakeweed, dropseed and Indian rice grass, plant names I'd learned back in school—names I never thought I'd recite inside my head as I close the distance between us, needing to ground myself with the very things that have sustained me. Mother Earth, Father Sky... and when I take her in my arms, my Sarah.

"Are you alright?" I pull her to me and hold her, feeling her body tremble against mine.

"Better now that you're here. He left twenty minutes ago but I couldn't go back. I wasn't sure if he'd be waiting." Her answer comes in gulps. I can feel her heart beating against my chest as I hold her. She seems so small, so delicate.

"Your car's totaled," I mumble as I pull away to inspect her face. Her left eye is swollen where he hit her and I swallow the curse threatening to come out of my mouth. I want nothing more than to kill the bastard for laying a hand on her, but she's safe she's safe she's safe. I pull Sarah to me again, holding her tightly as I fight back the tears from behind my eyelids. I pull away again, focusing. I need to check and make sure all of her is okay. I hold up her hands, her palms covered in scratches, pieces of earth stuck to the skin, blood caked in. Her knees and shins are covered in cuts, too.

"My ankle..." Sarah whispers as I get down on my haunches to get a closer look. Her left ankle is already swollen right above her sock, its elastic stretched to the maximum.

"Hang on, Sarah." I unlace her running shoes and slip off her sock as carefully as I can. Sarah cries out, her hands resting on my shoulder for support.

"Can you take me to the medical center? They'll know what to do," she says as I straighten up and hand her the shoe, the sock tucked inside. "I just hope I didn't break any bones."

I nod, lifting her in my arms. I don't want to say anymore. I just want to get her out of the sun and back to safety. Sarah buries face in my neck as I make my way slowly through the brush and back on the trail, each step evoking a mantra inside my head. Mother Earth, Father Sky, my Sarah.

When we reach the truck, I carefully set her down next to the passenger side and open the passenger side door.

"Oh, Benny, you brought me flowers."

My chest tightens when I see the sunflowers on the passenger seat. I'd completely forgotten about them. Then I remember what her neighbor said. Shit. What if Sarah had been home when Ryan came by her apartment yesterday?

Come to think of it, he wasn't carrying flowers.

The realization hits me like a punch to the gut and I take a deep breath. I stare at Sarah, fighting back the anger and rage for the man who can't let her go.

Get a grip, Benny. You can't lose it. Now now. Not ever.

Clearing my throat, I set the flowers on the floor and force a reassuring smile. "Let's get you to the hospital."

PEARL, Nana, and Dax arrive in Shiprock three hours later along with two members of their private security team. By then, Sarah is in my apartment asleep in my bed, her ankle iced and lathered in arnica gel we picked up from Central Market on the way.

While the security guys stay downstairs, the three of them cram into my small sofa until Nana gets up to head to the kitchen, telling everyone she needs to do something. Within minutes, she's done an inventory of my pots and pans and the contents of my refrigerator and asks me if she can make us all something to eat.

"Of course," I say. "Mi casa es su casa." As she clasps my hand, I can see the worry in her eyes. "Y la cocina tambien." *And the kitchen.*

Or I think I said it right.

"Daniel is on his way from New York," Pearl announces as she rises from the couch. Next to her, Dax follows, his expression distant. "I'd like to stay with her, if that's okay, Benny."

"Of course."

"Me, too," Dax mumbles, following his mother into my bedroom as I join Nana in the kitchen and help bring down a spice mix she spies from the cupboard.

"You have everything I need to make tacos," she says and I nod, smiling. Tacos are always good.

Daniel arrives just after midnight without any fanfare. It's a simple text message announcing he's downstairs and I let him in. The security guys are staying at a nearby motel and will be back in the morning. After all, it's not like we're expecting an attack or anything. I'd give my life for this family if I have to.

After a curt nod and a greeting, Daniel sets his carry-on bag next to the front door and looks at the apartment, his gaze on the couch where I'd been sleeping.

"I thought Sarah said you had a one-bedroom apartment," he says. "Where's everyone?"

"In here." I lead him into the bedroom, pushing the door partly open to reveal four sleeping figures on my king-sized bed. Never have I been more grateful to have one.

From left to right, it's Dax, Nana, Sarah, and Pearl. Sarah's ankle is elevated on a pillow, her sock-covered foot peeking out from under one of the blankets.

Beside me, Daniel chuckles. "Guess some things never change. You buy a five-bedroom house so everyone can have their own bedroom, and everyone sleeps in one bed anyway. At least, whenever I was away." Daniel turns to look at me. "How is she?"

"They gave her something for the pain and it knocked her out," I whisper as Daniel looks inside but doesn't walk in. "They've been with her since after we had dinner."

Daniel doesn't speak for a few moments. His Adam's apple bobs as he clears his throat. "Thank you, Benny."

From the bed, Pearl stirs.

"Daniel," she whispers as she carefully removes Sarah's arm draped over her chest and slides off the bed. As Daniel steps into the bedroom, I turn away, giving them the privacy they need as a family.

In the living room, my phone vibrates with an incoming text message from Tony.

Just got your message about taking the week off. Don't worry. We got everything covered at the office. Do what you need to do.

Thanks.

Hope your woman's alright.

I can't help but smile.

Your woman.

Guess everyone knows about that part, too. That's the thing with small towns. Everyone knows your business.

But it's not all bad. Just before her family arrived at my front door, Sarah and I learned that Ryan got pulled over for driving erratically on the highway. In the trunk of his car, they found a crowbar with pieces of glass that could only have come from Sarah's SUV. Sitting on the passenger seat next to him was her driver's license and credit cards that must have fallen out of her fanny pack when she ran.

He's being held at the detention center and will be charged with aggravated battery and causing bodily harm.

At the hospital, I'd learn that Ryan had followed Sarah on the trail after he smashed the windows but gave up when he couldn't find her. By then, she'd found a boulder to hide behind where she waited until she heard the sound of an engine starting. Only she was too scared to venture out, thinking he could still be waiting for her. She'd also twisted her ankle by then and knew she wouldn't be able to outrun him if he spotted her again. Sarah heard me calling out her name about twenty minutes later but even then, she thought she was hearing things. After all, I wasn't supposed to come home until tomorrow.

But that's how life works. Not everything goes according to plan and after everything that just happened, I'll take what I can get. Sarah is safe and with her family, and that's all I care about.

She's all I have.

CHAPTER TWENTY-THREE

Sarah

Two days later, I learn that Ryan is being charged with aggravated battery and causing bodily harm. There are other charges, too, but I barely hear what they are when Dad tells me after he returns from the courthouse. My face turns numb and I'm suddenly back at the trailhead, fending Ryan off. I want to tell Dad that I've seen firsthand what Ryan can do and my mind simply can't take anymore. No more replays, no more interviews by the detectives, no more questions. No more, no more, no more.

But Dad is being Dad. Someone tried to hurt his daughter and he'll go through hell to make sure Ryan will pay. He won't leave Shiprock until he's satisfied that Ryan will get his due. At least, it would mean that he wouldn't be near a computer for awhile even if there's nothing that can be done about all the pictures he posted. Like ripples on water, the consequences go far and wide.

I just want life to be normal again with Benny meeting me for a run after my shift followed by breakfast and then a quickie in the shower before he'd go to work and I'd crawl under the covers to sleep. But life isn't going to be the same again, not after this.

I can't even go back to work. The agency already notified me that they're not renewing my contract. At least, they didn't cite the morality clause as a reason this time, maybe on account of the attack on me that made the local papers. As far as everyone's concerned, my contract simply ran out and they have someone else flying in to do her 16-weeks.

But even if they would have extended my contract, it wouldn't have worked out. Word about my naked photos got out at the medical center not because of Ryan but Enrico. He found them while browsing porn sites and told a buddy who told another buddy who just happened to work at the medical center. I'm just grateful that it happened after I arrived at the emergency room and the detectives showing up right after to ask me questions and take my report. And since I don't have to come back to work because of my ankle, I won't have to go through the shame of having to deal with the whispers and the sideway glances. At least, Melina gave me that option even if she refuses to talk to me again.

With no prospect of a job for me in Shiprock, it means I have to return to Taos. It means leaving Benny who's gone above and beyond for my family and me.

He's never left my side since this all happened, not

once. And with my family now checked in at a local hotel, it's just us the moment they leave for the day. As Benny sleeps next to me, I touch his cheek, needing to memorize the feel of his beard on my fingers, the smooth skin along his cheekbone and the warm comfort of his breath, knowing he'll always be there for me.

He loves me.

For why else would he do everything he's done so far? Why else would he stay with me even after I disobeyed his advice not to run the trails by myself? And with the pictures now having made it to Shiprock, I can only imagine what his friends must be thinking.

His family.

"I'm sorry for everything," I whisper when he opens his eyes. "For Ryan, the pictures..."

"That's the past, Sarah. It's done. It's over. At least, you don't have to worry if anyone will ever know because now they do," he murmurs, taking my hand and pressing his mouth against my palm. "And wouldn't you know it, but the world didn't end."

I smile. "Why are you so positive?"

"Is there any other way to approach this?" He weaves his fingers with mine. "Some things are just out of our control whether it's Ryan finding you or Enrico spotting your pictures online and telling the world. At least, we know he's into porn, right?"

I roll my eyes. "What guy isn't?"

"Now you're painting all men with a wide brush, Sarah," he says with a look of mock seriousness.

"Although I have to admit, I've looked at my fair share when I was younger." He pauses. "The moment I got a good signal, that is."

We giggle, the seriousness of the last three days fading into memory. At least, for now. He pulls my hand toward him, our fingers still interlaced together.

"Come here."

I scoot closer to him and he unlaces his fingers from mine to give me room, making sure my sprained foot is also safely positioned over a pillow at our feet.

"You'd make a good nurse, you know," I say as I snuggle against his chest, his breath fanning the hair at the top of my head.

"Only for you, though," he murmurs. "I just want you safe, Sarah. That's all that matters."

"I don't want to be without you, Benny." I inhale his scent, taking him in. His strength. His raw masculinity. His soul.

"It'll be temporary," he says. "I'll put in for a transfer back to Taos and before you know it, you'll get sick of seeing me."

"I doubt it."

He chuckles. "That's good to know."

"But you're sad."

He swallows, his Adam's apple bobbing as I pull away to look at his face. I've been wanting to say those words since yesterday, after my family finally left his apartment and he drove me to mine where we've been ever since. It's in his eyes. It's in the way he sat on the couch yesterday staring at his phone. Just before I joined him, he turned it off but I saw the picture on the display before it went dark. His mother, sister, and two brothers. I don't even know their names for he's never told me.

"Tell me about your family," I asked him then and I could have sworn he tensed up before he forced a smile.

"Maybe another day," he replied. "I'd only bore you."

I smiled. "I doubt it."

He thought for a moment before shaking his head, his eyes sad. "Not right now, Sarah."

I knew then to let it go.

With everything that happened, I need to focus only on Ryan and making sure he's charged for his crimes. Maybe after all this, Benny will finally tell me. But until then, I'll have to wait until he's ready.

"So what's the plan today?" He asks a few minutes later. "Do you need help packing?"

"I think my mom and Nana have that task down like the pros that they are," I say, giggling. "I had to make sure my...um, personal toys were out of the way before they found it."

"What about the bars under the bed? Leather straps and everything?" Benny asks and I stare at him, my eyes, wide. "I mean, we have had three straight weeks of playing and testing them out before you went out of commission."

I laugh, burying my face in his chest. "Just wait until I'm back in commission again."

"We better get off the bed so I can take them out. I'll install them in my place in Taos."

I look up at him. "Planning ahead?"

He grins. "Of course. The doctor did say four weeks before you can do anything, um, strenuous."

I bite my lip, my hand drifting lower to press against his erection. "Well, the way I see it, I'm not the one who's going to be doing anything strenuous."

"You're right."

Benny closes his eyes as my hand slips under his boxers to stroke him. "Besides, after all the excitement the past few days, I've been... how shall you say it... feeling a bit neglected."

"How neglected?"

I squeeze his shaft, running my palm over the head of his cock, pre-cum already coating the tip. "This neglected."

"Are you sure that's not painkillers talking?"

"No, I want the pain. Your kind of pain, the one only you can deliver," I whisper, kissing his tattooed chest, my hand stroking him, squeezing him.

"Be careful what you wish for," he murmurs. "We'll be doing acrobatics with that ankle of yours in a minute."

I look up at him, hunger darkening his gaze. "Is that a promise?"

"Oh, definitely, princess. I'll have that ankle of yours up to your ear very soon."

I bite my lip, giggling. "I'm waiting."

"You're bad. What happened to my obedient sub."

"Guess you'll have to check on her and find out. I hear she can be very naughty sometimes. She can be a brat, actually." I giggle when Benny lowers his head, his beard tickling my neck.

"Oh, I know that very well," he murmurs, kissing my neck and the skin behind my ear, giving me goosebumps. "In fact, I just might need to do something about that right now."

As he rolls me onto my back, making sure he doesn't bump my ankle, I find myself feeling much lighter than when I woke up this morning. Butterflies flutter inside my belly as Benny's hand pushes my oversized t-shirt aside to cup my breast, rolling a nipple between his thumb and index finger, his mouth on mine, his tongue already tasting me.

As he moves down my neck, his hand drifts lower down my belly to the heat between my legs. I barely remember the throbbing in my injured ankle, all sensations concentrated wherever his mouth descends. My mound, my folds, my sensitive clit.

"Benny..."

"You better text your mom and tell her not to come too early," he murmurs before kissing the skin inside my thigh. "Or she'll be in for a surprise."

I glance at the clock, realizing he's right, and reach for my phone on the bedside table. I gasp when he sucks on my clit and slides a finger inside me.

"You taste so fucking good." He slides another finger

inside me and I moan, the simple act of typing out a text message suddenly difficult.

Can u come an hour later?

Benny's tongue feels exquisite and I rest my phone on my chest as he locks my hips down on the bed with his arms, the sound of my moans filling the room.

Sure. Breakfast burritos okay? Green chile?

Yes. Just don't come yet.

I chuckle as I let the phone drop on the side of the bed, not waiting for a reply. Surely Mom will understand.

"They got the message?" Benny slips a third finger in and I arch my back, closing my eyes as his tongue laps at my folds.

"Yes... and they'll bring breakfast burritos... oh, God, Benny..." I turn my head to the side, burying my face in a pillow as my orgasm builds. "Oh, and green chile."

"Is that your safe word?"

I glare at him, fighting back the giggle that almost ruins the moment. Benny grins and lowers his head and I gasp as he sucks on my clit again, his fingers moving in and out of me, driving me to the brink.

He molds his mouth to my pussy, his fingers

corkscrewing in and out of me. I can't take anymore. I want him inside me.

"Fuck me, Benny. I can't take anymore."

His dark eyes gaze up at me. It's so primal, so carnal, and I love it. I look down at him, my fingers gripping his hair. "You forgot something, Sarah."

"Please fuck me, Sir," I gasp and like a magic code word, he moves up, kissing the heated skin of my belly, my breasts, and then my mouth, his tongue giving me a taste of myself as he presses the head of his cock at my entrance.

"Say it again," he murmurs and as I do, Benny thrusts deep and hard, filling me completely, his lips capturing my scream. His roughness in bed is what I crave. It ignites, it quenches, it consumes me. As he watches me, his eyes darken, the part of him that I awoke that one night come to life. My salvation. My everything.

"Benny..." His name becomes a mantra I repeat again and again as he slides in and out of me, filling me, driving me to the edge and back. Nothing held back because there's nothing left to be held back. I've given him everything.

Benny captures my wrists and pins them to the bed over my head. His mouth descends on mine, swallowing his name as it escapes from my lips. I can feel my orgasm building, burning through me, a tight wet heat that propels me to the very brink.

"Ben–" His hand covers my mouth as I come, his name muffled against his palm. This is how it's going to be for us, the push and pull of my submission and his domination, a continuing exploration of a dynamic we want together.

Two years after I first asked him, Benny gave me everything I wanted.

"Sarah..." When his own release comes, the sound of my name from his lips is like a drug I can't be without from this moment on. The way he looks at me, the way he holds me, the way he claims me like this is like the air I breathe. I want him. I crave him.

I love him.

EPILOGUE

Benny

Dax emerges from the garage as I park my truck in their driveway. The kid's arms are covered in sawdust from whatever he's making but he's got a huge grin on his face as he walks toward me.

"Tell me if you can spot the nails." He hands me a smooth wooden box. It's light in my hand, its edges sanded smooth and even.

"There are no nails."

"Glue?" He persists. "Where did I glue it together? Can you spot it?"

I want to tell him he didn't use any glue because he fit the box together using Japanese joinery. But that would only bring the poor kid down. His excitement is palpable.

"Here." I point to a spot where the longer piece joined up with the shorter ends. "You glued them here."

"Nope!" Dax grins as I hand him back the box. "I

used joints. Japanese joints. They're called sashi…wait, sashi something."

"Sashimono," I say as Dax nods.

"I checked out that Japanese guy you told me and Dad about and his work is amazing. Long waiting list," Dax says. "Dad ordered a piece for his office and it'll take the guy over a year to make it. Isn't that crazy? But Dad's gonna wait."

"Wouldn't you wait if you knew it'll be one of the most beautiful things you'll have in your office?"

Dax shrugs. "I guess."

"Does he have apprenticeships available?"

"He says I'm not ready," Dax replies, exhaling. "A bummer, but Dad says he's right. Takeshi-san. That's his name. You add the 'san' at the end as a sign of respect, you see."

"One day soon you'll be ready, though, right?" I say, doing my best to be hopeful even as my stomach is growling at the aromas drifting from the house. Green chile is definitely on the menu today.

"Yeah. He says I can hang out at his workshop in the meantime, but he can't take me on as an apprentice right away," Dax says. "Dad says I have to earn it. Like making tea for the kung-fu masters, like in those Jackie Chan movies."

"So you ready to make tea for the next few years before Takeshi-san decides you can be his apprentice?"

Dax thinks for a moment, studying the wooden box in his hands. "I think I am. It'll keep me out of trouble, that's for sure. And Dad will be happy I'm not just sitting around my room playing video games all day."

"Benny, I could have sworn I heard you arrive," Pearl says from the garage door leading into the house. "Come in. And Dax, shower up before you join us at the table. You've been out here since morning."

"Ask him if he even brushed his teeth before going out to the garage this morning," a sassy voice retorts from inside the house as Dax rolls his eyes.

"She's back to her usual annoying self, you know, my sister," he mutters. "So good luck, man. You're gonna need it."

I chuckle as Sarah emerges from behind her mother, screaming my name as she runs toward me. There's a very slight limp in her gait but her ankle is finally healed.

As she flings herself into my arms, I can't believe it's been a month since I last saw her, that last time we barely left my bedroom for two days. Maybe that's why her parents decided to have me over for lunch first before I whisk their daughter away to my little fortress across town.

I barely hear Dax saying he'll see me inside. All I can hear and see and feel is my sassy and (according to her brother) annoying woman in my arms. She smells of chile, flour and sage, a weird combination but I like it.

"So that's why you wanted that wild sage bread recipe from me last week," I murmur as I put her down and pick a piece of dried sage from her hair. The recipe had been my mother's, one I'd written down for Noelle a long time ago although she never got around to making it.

"I'm in charge of the bread since I can't seem to cook anything else. I can't handle any smells of meat right now," she says, taking my hand and guiding me into the house through the garage. "But it's because I've been cooped up inside the house since I left Shiprock. I can't wait to go back to work but Dad's not so sure yet. We still have crazies hanging outside the gate so we can't let the security guys go. Not that they probably want to leave, they're both starting to gain weight from Nana's cooking."

I laugh, Sarah's excitement so evident as she rattles on. Now I understand why Daniel keeps in shape. You have to with all the delicious dishes his mother-in-law and wife make whenever he's home. Someone should have warned the security detail.

As we step inside the house, no one needs to tell me what's on the menu. My stomach growls at the aromas wafting from the kitchen, of chile stew with corn dumplings, green corn pudding and Sarah's wild sage bread. Wanna bet, there's probably also a plate full of sopapillas because they're a staple in the Drexel household.

Like fry bread.

My chest tightens and I'm suddenly somewhere else.

Shi'ma standing in front of the stove. My grandparents shucking corn. Marjorie setting the dishes on the table. Tahoma and Tsela arguing on the couch over whose turn it is to play next. Even Ray, in a rare sober moment, walking behind his wife to give her a pat on the rear.

My jaw clenches. My mouth turns dry.

Twice, I'd driven to the homestead only to have my twin brothers awkwardly standing outside, tasked with the job of telling me I'm no longer welcome. They wouldn't even take the jugs of water I'd brought with me, the bags of groceries I'd bought for everyone.

We're not even allowed to talk to you, Tsela mumbled, avoiding my gaze. *Dad will get really mad at us.*

And he's watching us, so just leave, bro. Don't make it hard for us, Tahoma said.

And that's what I did, not needing a third attempt to get their message.

I'm not wanted. Not anymore.

"Hey." Sarah tugs arm. "You okay?"

I clear my throat. "Yeah, I'm fine. Just... taking in everything." I squeeze her hand and smile. "I can't wait to taste the bread you made."

Sarah's eyes narrow as she gazes at me, as if unconvinced, but only for a moment. She wraps her arms around my neck, burying her face in my chest. I kiss the top of her head, inhaling the scent of sage and flour, my arms tightening around her.

"Thank you, Sarah."

She doesn't say anything and it's enough. She knows. She understands.

"Hey, you two. Ready for lunch?" Daniel asks as I pull away and shake his hand. He's casual Dad today, dressed in a plaid shirt over a white t-shirt and khaki pants.

"Yup." From the corner of my eye, I can see the two security guys in the kitchen, one of them tasting something from a spoon that Nana is holding up to his mouth. He gives her the thumbs up and I chuckle. Sarah was right. They're starting to gain weight.

"Sarah here told us what your favorite dishes were," Pearl says from the kitchen. "We'd already had posole the other night so we had to come up with something else."

"Hope you like it," Nana says in heavily accented English.

"Oh, I will, Nana," I say, laughing. "I made sure to come hungry."

The door from the garage opens and Gabe behind me.

"Whoa!" Daniel exclaims as Gabe shakes my hand. "Where'd you come from?"

"The garage door was open so I just walked in," he says as Daniel presses the button to close it. "Hope Dax asked you first, Uncle Dan, but he called and asked me to come over. Said he didn't want to be the only one under twenty-one in here. Said he's surrounded by oldies."

We all laugh as Gabe shrugs, disappearing in the direction of the bedrooms.

"The kid knows he's always welcome in here just as

you are, too, Benny," Daniel says, ushering Sarah and me toward the table. "Grab a seat."

"I need to wash up first."

"Me, too. We'll be right back." Sarah grabs my hand and guides me toward the hallway leading to the guest bathroom.

"You two don't take too long in there," Pearl says as Sarah walks past the bathroom and right into the study, pulling me right behind her. The moment we're both inside, she closes the door and steps right back into my arms again. This time, our lips meet and the hollowness that had been in my chest just moments earlier fades away, the emptiness that had come with the memories of my family replaced with all the love I could ever want in her arms.

I draw away and stroke her face, as if needing to make sure she's real. Her temples, her cheekbones, my thumb tracing her full lips that widen in a smile. Sarah looks radiant, her blue eyes sparkling as she gazes up at me.

"I have something to tell you."

"Yes?"

"The bathroom wasn't the best place to do it but I can't wait anymore." She takes my hand and brings it lower, past her breasts and letting it rest over her belly. "I think it was the painkillers that did it. Made it fail."

I frown, her belly warm against my palm. "Made what fail?"

"The pill," she whispers, biting her lip. "I'm pregnant, Benny."

The words echo inside my head as I stare at her. "What?"

"Two months," she continues as the words finally make sense and I can't breathe.

"Are you serious?"

She suddenly looks scared. "I'm sorry. I think me being on the painkillers made the pill fail and—"

I pull her to me, no longer hearing anything else she's saying as I hold her tightly, not wanting to let go. Tears prick my eyelids. "We're pregnant," I murmur against her neck. "We're pregnant, Sarah."

Her body relaxes in my arms. "So you're okay with it?"

I look at her in wonderment. "Why wouldn't I be okay with it? You're pregnant. We're going to have a baby."

"Yes, we are." She wipes the tears that cling to my eyelashes, her voice breaking as she continues. "Oh, Benny, now you're making me cry, too, and wanna bet, when we tell them later, my mom's gonna cry buckets."

"I won't tell anyone."

We laugh at our silliness, at our shock and seconds later, at the fresh tears rolling down our faces as we do our best to tell ourselves to get a grip.

"We have to tell them, Benny," she says, cocking her head toward the door. "Together."

I pull her to me and kiss her, tasting the salty taste of her tears on her lips. "Together."

Minutes later, we join everyone in the dining room together, a Mona Lisa smile on Sarah's face as she clears her throat and everyone stops what they're doing and looks at us. It takes Pearl three seconds, tops, to guess the news, her eyes widening as she looks from Sarah to me and down to where Sarah's hand rests on her belly.

"Is it true? You're pregnant?"

"Yes," Sarah replies and that's all it takes before sweet pandemonium ensues. Nana, Pearl, and Daniel surround us with their hugs and congratulations, tears optional although like Sarah warned me minutes earlier, her mother is crying buckets. Even Dax and Gabe come downstairs to find out what the fuss is all about and I see Dax's face go from shock to amazement to awe as he processes the news that his sister is going to be a mother.

But Dax isn't the only one with things to process. As Daniel claps my shoulder and pulls me in a tight embrace, it takes all my willpower not to break down in front of everyone as it finally hits me. This is my family... and I'm home.

I'm finally home.

THE END... FOR NOW

Thank you so much for reading **Other Side of Love**. I hope you enjoyed Sarah and Benny's story as much I loved writing it. There's definitely more to come with these two.

If this is your first time inside the world of the Drexels and their friends, I hope you'll check out the other couples in the series.

Everything She Ever Wanted
Dax and Harlow

Falling for Jordan
Addison and Jordan

Breaking the Rules
Sawyer and Alma

Friends with Benefits
Campbell and Caitlin

To keep up with the latest stories I'm working on, you can sign up for my newsletter by visiting *lizdurano.com/subscribe*

ACKNOWLEDGMENTS

This book wouldn't have been possible if not for the readers who believed in Sarah and Benny and the world that is *A Different Kind of Love*. Thank you for believing in me to tell it at the right time.

Thank you to Charity Chimni and Michelle Jo Quinn for being the best cheerleaders this writer could ask for. Those gentle nudges do help a lot...as are the reminders not to buy any more premade covers. My gratitude also goes to the ladies of Kworki for their unrelenting encouragement and positivity. You know who you are.

To my family and most especially my son who never stops believing in me and to whom this book is dedicated to (because he declared it and rightly so), my eternal gratitude. Thank you for allowing me to write my stories and for letting me talk to myself when I need to.

OTHER BOOKS BY LIZ DURANO

A Different Kind of Love

Everything She Ever Wanted

Breaking the Rules

Falling for Jordan

Friends with Benefits

Holiday Engagement Series

The Replacement Fiancé

The Reluctant Fiancee

The Last Minute Fiancé

Celebrity Series

Loving Ashe

Loving Riley

California Love

Finding Sam

In His Heart

Fire and Ice

Collateral Attraction

ABOUT THE AUTHOR

Liz grew up devouring fairy tales and her mother's book collection (don't tell her!) that included Harold Robbins, James Clavell, and Colleen McCullough. Although she studied Journalism in college, she discovered that she preferred writing fiction and so these days, that's what she does. She writes women's fiction and romance and lives in Southern California with her family and a Chihuahua mix who keeps guard of her writing space.

You can follow Liz's book adventures by visiting lizdurano.com or follow her on Facebook at @lizduranobooks

Or visit my Reader Group where I share new chapters and the latest news:
https://www.facebook.com/
groups/librarycafereadergroup/

CPSIA information can be obtained
at www.ICGtesting.com
Printed in the USA
LVHW090323130421
684335LV00007B/50

9 780986 284762